LADY GOLD INVESTIGATES VOLUME 4

CHRISTMAS EDITION

LEE STRAUSS
NORM STRAUSS

Library and Archives Canada Cataloguing in Publication

Title: Lady Gold Investigates Volume 4 : a short read cozy historical 1920s mystery collection / Lee Strauss.

Names: Strauss, Lee (Novelist), author.

Description: Short stories. | Contents: v. 4. The Case of the Haunted Castle -- The Case of the Missing Christmas Goose.

Identifiers: Canadiana (print) 20190131608 | Canadiana (ebook) 20190131624 | ISBN 9781774091357 (v. 4 :

hardcover) | ISBN 9781774091364 (v. 4 : softcover) | ISBN 9781774091371 (v. 4 : IngramSpark softcover) |

ISBN 9781774091333 (v. 4 : Kindle) | ISBN 9781774091340 (v. 4 : EPUB)

Classification: LCC PS8637.T739 L34 2019 | DDC C813/.6—dc23

THE CASE OF THE HAUNTED CASTLE

LADY GOLD INVESTIGATES STORIES ARE
SET IN THE YEAR 1925.

1

———

With a blast of a blustery December wind, Basil and Ginger Reed arrived on schedule at Edinburgh's Waverley Station. They, along with their beloved Boston Terrier aptly named *Boss*, had left King's Cross Station in London just over eight hours earlier and the trip had been a wonderful reminder of their wedding journey two years before. Only this time, thankfully, they didn't have the intrigue of a dead body and a murder case to solve.

Ginger wore her slate-blue silk marocain coat that had sleeves and a hem stitched in curved scallops and tightened the snowy-white ermine collar around her neck. Basil waved down a taxicab. "The Baron's Hotel, please."

"Yes, sir." The taxicab driver smiled at Boss, who, lulled by the rhythmic chugging of the train, had slept most of the way and was now wide awake and panting happily, his stubby tail wagging. Once Ginger was seated, Boss stood with his hind legs on her lap, his front legs perched on the sill of the taxi door, watching everything go by with keen interest.

Edinburgh was as enchanting as ever, and Ginger once again marvelled at the city's almost theatrical beauty with its tall spires of dark stone and magnificent network of crescents, streets, and terraces. It almost seemed that some of the older sections of the city, dominated by Edinburgh Castle, were literally hewn out of the rocky crags and cliffs that overlooked the newer parts of the city built on the plain below. Now, as the evening darkness closed in, many of the great old buildings were lit up by gas lights, giving the city an even more dramatic and gothic appearance.

Soon the taxicab came to a stop and Basil paid the driver as Ginger took in the Permian sandstone façade of The Baron's Hotel. Stamped with the date 1903, the building was comparatively new, and the marble-floored lobby added a touch of sophistication.

Their room had an unobstructed view of Edinburgh Castle and the markets below. The travel weariness Ginger had felt after stepping off the train vanished as she gazed at the sights, and she was suddenly energized to jump right in.

Turning to Basil she said, "Let's go for a walk in the old town before turning in for the night."

"Fabulous idea, love," he returned.

Leading Boss on his leash, they walked slowly arm in arm through quiet lantern-lit streets, Boss' claws clicking softly on the cobblestones. Most of the shops were closed for the night so few people mingled about. Snowflakes fell in a slow, delicate dance.

"Thank you for joining me on this trip, Ginger," Basil said. "I know I've already thanked you, but tonight, walking with you through these splendid surroundings, I'm newly reminded of what a lucky chap I am."

Ginger leaned over and gave him a peck on the cheek. "It's entirely my pleasure."

When Basil had proposed that she come to Edinburgh with him she was all too happy to accept. As an esteemed chief inspector at Scotland Yard, Basil was in Edinburgh to train the city's up-and-coming police detectives. Subjects to be lectured on included the latest techniques in fingerprint detection, what was new in forensics, and how to work with the medical examiner, along with general police department management.

As a private investigator, Ginger was keenly interested in the latest in police procedures, and she and Basil discussed the topic thoroughly many evenings over a glass of brandy, sitting beside the fireplace at Hartigan House.

"Lecturing a bunch of bored constables is not exactly a grand adventure," Basil said.

"They will not be bored!" Ginger poked him in the ribs. "I am sure you will prove to be a very engaging lecturer, and I have no doubt the lot of them will soon fall under your professorial spell."

"Professorial spell!" Basil laughed. "Now that would be a trick wouldn't it?"

"I am very proud of you, you know." Ginger put her head on his shoulder for a moment as they walked.

The training sessions took place in a rented conference room in another hotel. It was close enough to where they were staying that Basil could simply walk there after breakfasting, so long as he wore his boots and bundled up in a wool coat and scarf. The next morning, he finished his cup of tea, then reached over to tuck a stray strand of Ginger's red bob behind her ear.

"Please consider dropping in to one of the sessions," he implored. "I would love to introduce you. I look very much more handsome with you on my arm."

"You certainly do, Chief Inspector." Ginger's green eyes sparkled as she teased her husband.

"On Thursday, they want me to consult on some challenging cases that they have on file," Basil added. "That will probably be the most interesting thing that happens all week." He shook his head. "Apparently, there has been a spate of art thefts that have gone unsolved."

"That sounds absolutely fascinating," Ginger said, yawning for effect. "I will consider the offer if my schedule allows."

Basil looked at her and then grinned. "You're teasing me."

"What? I wouldn't." She fluttered her eyelids innocently and then laughed.

Ginger was looking forward to empty days spending time exploring some of the interesting nooks and crannies of Edinburgh at a leisurely pace, and of course, doing a bit of Christmas shopping.

"If I don't turn up, we'll meet for dinner," she said. "Somewhere romantic."

"I'll look forward to it."

He kissed her and waved goodbye as he placed his trilby on his head and put on his winter coat.

As Ginger finished her breakfast, she noticed a well-dressed young man staring at her from across the room. She made sure her wedding band was clearly visible, making a point of waving her long fingers towards the waiter. "Another coffee, please."

Her demonstration did nothing to sway the man from leaving his table and approaching her, his black patent-leather Oxford shoes echoing off the marble floor. Ginger smiled politely.

The man had the nerve to sit in Basil's empty chair, and without invitation! In his late twenties, he was handsome, with a ruddy face and thick blond hair, which he wore slicked back and parted on one side. He presented a casual affluence without the arrogance that money can often bring.

"Excuse me," he said, removing his hat. "Are you Lady Gold?"

2

———————

Ginger lowered her coffee cup, holding in her feeling of surprise. As far as she knew, no one outside her family, staff, and close friends knew she was in Edinburgh. To have her name, her formal name no less, called out in public so far from her home setting was rather startling.

Although, she had been known to make the society pages on occasion, so perhaps he'd spotted her in a rare photograph.

"Yes, I am," Ginger replied politely. "Though I go by Mrs. Reed now. Who, may I ask, are you?"

"I'm sorry," he replied, his Scottish brogue not nearly as severe as some others Ginger had heard. "My manners seem to have left me for a moment." He stretched out his hand. "I'm very honoured to meet you. My name is Charles McCallum."

Ginger noted his long fingers and well-manicured fingernails. "How do you do?" she said.

A waiter approached their table. "Are you joining the lady, sir?"

"No, I'm only saying hello."

"I'm about to leave as well," Ginger said. "Please charge my and my husband's breakfast to our room."

She grinned at her guest, hoping he would catch the emphasis on the word, "husband".

When the waiter left them, Mr. McCallum continued. "I do apologise for approaching unannounced like this, but it really is serendipitous. Lady Gold, er, Mrs. Reed, I have a proposal for you."

Ginger's curiosity was quite stirred, and she waited with anticipation of what the man could possibly want from her. Though she was quite eager to shop, the frocks and shoes could wait.

"My older brother is Walter McCallum, a senior police officer here in Edinburgh."

"Ah, then he will be acquainted with my husband, Chief Inspector Reed. He's advising the Edinburgh police force this week. It's the reason for our visit."

"Tremendous, yes. It was Walter who first told me about Lady Gold Investigations—your reputation does precede you."

Ginger felt flushed with the praise. "That certainly does my ego good, Mr. McCallum."

"Yes, well, I'll get to the point then. Do you believe in ghosts?"

Ginger blinked. Mr. McCallum had certainly shocked her with his enquiry. "No, I do not."

"Good then, we are on the right track."

Ginger smiled wryly. "What a relief."

"Yes, well, you see, Mrs. Reed, I have recently inherited a haunted castle. Kirksbridge Castle isn't large as far as castles go and is rather run-down and in ruins. But it is gaining a reputation, and not the type that I favour."

"It has ghosts?" Ginger asked.

"Yes, well... no. I mean I don't think so, but that's the problem, you see. I don't believe in ghosts, but unfortunately those ghosts that I don't believe in are causing me a lot of bother and costing me a fair penny as well."

"How do you mean?" Ginger asked, intrigued.

"The castle has been in the family for many generations, but virtually abandoned for the last twenty-five years. My great uncle Gilbert McCallum lived in a small section of it and let the rest of the building languish. A lonely bachelor who never married, he thought he could make a go of it by turning the castle into a hotel. Unfortunately, ill-fortune befell his entire estate through the war years and he never did make anything of it for want of money."

Mr. McCallum sighed then finished his exposé by saying, "When Uncle Gilbert passed away, the deed to Kirksbridge Castle was passed on to me."

"How interesting," Ginger said. "What are your plans for the castle now?"

"Well, that's just it. I thought I'd finish what my uncle started and employed a renovation crew from Perth. It took me a while to find a crew willing to work on the place. Anyway, the plan was to open up the parts of the castle that are newly refurbished to hotel guests as the repairs allowed. We've finished about half of the castle now, but the crew that was employed to do the final work is too spooked to finish the job. And I can't seem to keep any guests in the place for more than one night."

"Why is that?" Ginger asked.

"Strange goings-on."

Ginger leaned in. "Like what, Mr. McCallum?"

"Oh, Lady Gold, this list is long. Strange noises at night for one, like chains rattling on the floor. Then there's the sudden temperature changes in a room. Objects being moved from their place and put on the opposite side of the building during the night. Pets of the guests suddenly becoming very frightened and hiding under the bed."

Ginger thought about Boss, waiting patiently in their room. It was hard for her to imagine him being frightened by anything like that. Hiding under the bed was definitely not his style.

"I'm sure all of those things could be explained," Ginger offered.

Mr. McCallum snorted. "There's more. A few weeks ago, members of the crew were frightened by a strange apparition hovering in the library, in which they were just beginning to do their work. They claimed to have seen the ghostly form of a woman in a flowing dress. This was moments after the lamps in the room had all suddenly gone out because of an unexplained wind. Apparently, the woman had a horribly disfigured face. The crew refused to return to work after that, and all work has been halted."

Ginger placed long fingernails against her lips. "Oh mercy."

"Three weeks ago, a couple was sleeping in one of the finished rooms when they heard a strange noise. The husband went downstairs to investigate and ended up in the same room where the workers had seen the apparition. Sure enough, it suddenly appeared before him too." Mr. McCallum blew air out of his cheeks in frustration. "There was no way for me to convince them to stay another night. Unfortunately, the man is on the town council in Dunblane, a burgh up near Stirling. You can imagine the stories he told his colleagues when he got back. What I was hoping to be a favourable review turned out to be an embarrassment."

"I see your problem," Ginger said, sympathising. "Have you ever spent the night there?"

"Oh yes, I live there with my wife in the same section that my Uncle Gilbert once lived in."

"And?"

Mr. McCallum hesitated before answering. "Last night I heard what sounded like scraping and digging coming from what used to be the castle dungeon. I was just above it in one of the ground-floor storerooms taking stock of our food items. I lit a lantern and headed down the old wooden steps that lead to the cellar." He stared at Ginger intently, then ran a hand through his thick hair.

"Go on," Ginger prompted.

Charles McCallum let out a tired breath. "I heard cackling."

"*Cackling?*" Ginger asked.

"Yes. Evil cackling. Like a witch or a hag, mocking and threatening me at the same time. I have to admit it got the better of me. I couldn't work up the courage to go down there until this morning."

"And what did you find?"

Mr. McCallum lifted a shoulder. "Nothing out of the ordinary."

Ginger inclined her head. "Have you told the police?"

"I told Walter. He's begged me not to make an official complaint. Said I'd make our family name a laughing stock."

"So, what do you want from me?" Ginger asked.

"I'm at my wits' end, Mrs. Reed," Mr. McCallum let out a distressing sigh. "If I don't find a solution soon, I'm going to have to abandon my plans for the hotel. Please, Lady Gold, will you take the case and help me find the ghost of Kirksbridge Castle?"

3

───────

It had only taken her a moment to consider whether or not to take the case, especially when Mr. McCallum sweetened the deal by offering the use of his 1924 Austin, which was much like the motorcar Basil drove.

"It'll be all right if I bring my dog, Boss, with me presumably," she said sweetly. "I'd hate to leave him alone in the room for the day."

"That's fine by me." Her new client smirked. "So long as he doesn't scare the ghosts away."

"But I thought that was what you wanted," Ginger said with a hint of a tease.

"By golly, you're right. Your *Boss* might just save my bacon!"

Speaking of bacon, Ginger had remembered to tuck a couple of pieces into her napkin to give to Boss. What an exciting day her pet had ahead of him now!

After returning to her room, Ginger changed from her morning dress into something more suitable for gallivanting about castle ruins.

She removed a winter-white frock with a yoked skirt and joined pleated section from the hotel wardrobe. She paired it with a blue Kasha jacket trimmed with red piping, a matching belt, and a contrasting tan and red crêpe de Chine scarf. "What do you think of this, Bossy?"

Boss, sitting on his haunches, licked the last of the bacon grease from his black lips. His brown eyes sparkled with approval.

"I think so too."

Ginger dressed, tucked her red bob under a woollen hat, and applied soft-pink lipstick. With Boss under her arm, she approached the lobby and spoke to the valet who assured her that the motorcar in question was indeed waiting for her.

Kirksbridge Castle did not fail to disappoint Ginger as she drove the Austin out of the city and up to the castle grounds, carefully following Mr. McCallum's directions. He was to meet her there since he had business to attend to in Edinburgh, and he didn't know exactly how long it would take. The late morning was very grey and dense with winter fog, and the castle suddenly loomed in front of her, appearing like a huge, lost ship sailing through thick ocean mists. The castle was four storeys high in a rough L-shaped configuration with a circular tower built in the inner corner where the two wings met. Mr. McCallum had been right in describing it as a small castle; it was not much larger than a mansion. Instead of a sprawling building with many wings, it was a towering, narrow-looking building. Ginger had read Bram Stoker's *Dracula* several years ago, and it seemed to her that Kirksbridge Castle would have been an inspiring place for the Irish author to write that chilling novel.

The garden surrounding the seventeenth-century structure was dusted in snow and did indeed look abandoned. Mr. McCallum had given Ginger a pamphlet that contained a short written history of the castle. He had had it printed for guests of the castle hotel to read and thought that it might help Ginger with the investigation.

Built between 1609 and 1615 by Sir Felix Buchanan, the

seventh laird of the surrounding county, the castle was situated a few miles from the nearest village but still very much out in the country. It featured a vaulted ground floor with two unvaulted upper storeys and a rebuilt garret. Beneath the castle was a dungeon.

According to local lore, the "ghost" that haunted the castle could be Lady McBain. The visiting noblewoman had been murdered on Christmas Day in 1795 by a jealous groundskeeper with whom she had had an affair and then subsequently spurned. Apparently, the rebuffed man had attacked his lover with pruning shears, then locked her in the dungeon to die. Her family thought she'd had a mental episode and run off, possibly into the sea and drowned, until her bones were discovered years later.

The castle had various turrets with conical roofs and Ginger spied several peep holes and pistol holes as she and Boss strolled around the edifice.

"Can I help ye, miss?"

Approaching from behind her, was a man with a thin, long nose and close-set eyes that regarded her with suspicion from under grey, bushy eyebrows. He wore a blue cap on what appeared to be a bald head, and his grey groundskeeper's trousers had dirt stains on one knee.

Ginger waved. "Hello. I'm Mrs. Ginger Reed, visiting from London."

"Yer a long way from home, madam," he said. "I'm afraid we're not accustomed to people walkin' about the grounds without first checkin' in with the management."

"Actually, I've been personally invited by Mr. Charles McCallum. He said he would meet me here shortly." Ginger glanced at her wristwatch to make a point.

"Oh, I see," the man said. "I do apologise, madam. We're a wee bit protective of the place since all this...trouble began. I'm Harold Macleod, the chief groundskeeper." He grinned at Ginger, revealing crooked front teeth. His canines actually resembled small fangs, and when he smiled, he suddenly took on the appearance of some kind of figure from that Bram Stoker novel the castle had brought to mind. If dressed in a black cape, the look would have been convincing.

The man continued, "So ye know about the... ghostin's, then?"

"Mr. McCallum did mention that." Ginger considered the older man. "What do you think of the haunting?"

"*Well.*" Mr. Macleod lifted his hat, ran a hand over his balding head and plopped the hat back on. "I think it's very peculiar, now that yer askin'."

"You haven't seen anything yourself?"

Mr. Macleod hesitated. "There's been a few strange things, all right."

"Like what?"

"Things movin' around in the middle of the night, for starters. Guests bein' scared out of their wits and leavin' without even askin' for their money back. Strange smells suddenly comin' into the room. Fog appearin' out o' nowhere. Mr. McCallum himself heard a cacklin' sound comin' from the dungeon."

"Have you been in the dungeon recently?" Ginger asked.

"Oh no!" Mr. Macleod said. "I got no interest to go down there."

"When did these, er, ghostings start?" Ginger asked.

"Well, I don't like to speak out of turn, but they did seem to get more frequent after our guest arrived."

"Guest?" Ginger said. "Singular?"

"Yes, madam. One gentleman. Now, I really shouldn't be talkin' about our guests to strangers." His eyes flashed with regret. "I've spouted off too much already."

"I'm sure it's all right," Ginger said kindly. "Mr. McCallum asked me to visit the castle precisely so I could investigate the haunting."

Mr. Macleod stared back warily. "Are ye another journalist?"

"*Another* journalist?" Ginger returned.

"The man in room five," Mr. Macleod said. "Name's Alfred Ferguson. He's a journalist of sorts."

"What do you mean?"

"Well, I think I would put him squarely in the category of those bloody 'jazz journalists', ye know, the ones who blow things up far beyond their proportion to try to make a big story. I dinna ken why Mr. McCallum lets him stay here, to be honest. He works for that newspaper *The Glasgow Telegraph*; a rag filled with nonsensical blether as far as I'm concerned." The groundskeeper pulled a red handkerchief out of his pocket and ran it under his birdlike nose. "He's probably writin' a story as we speak, up in his room with his typing machine." He stuffed the handkerchief into his breast pocket. "And his fancy perfumes." He rolled his eyes as if some rancid odour had suddenly appeared, and Ginger remembered Charles McCallum's reference to strange smells.

"He'll write some big story about ghosts at Kirksbridge..." Mr. Macleod continued, "...and soon after, my wife and me will be out of a job! No one will want to stay in a haunted castle!"

Ginger wondered if the opposite might be true. She also wondered why Charles McCallum had failed to mention anything about a reporter staying at the castle or why he would tolerate a sensationalist journalist during this time.

The sound of a car approaching reached them around the front of the castle.

"That must be Mr. McCallum," Mr. Macleod said, and gestured for Ginger to meet the car.

4

———

*M*r. Macleod had disappeared inside the castle before Mr. McCallum exited his motorcar.

"Thank goodness my business with the tax office in Edinburgh only took a few minutes," he said cheerily. "Did you get a chance to look around a bit?"

"Not really," Ginger said. "I just met your groundskeeper, though."

Mr. McCallum chuckled. "Nice fella, if a bit chatty. Allow me to give you a tour, Mrs. Reed."

Ginger scooped up Boss and followed Mr. McCallum through massive weathered wooden doors with rusted wrought-iron hinges that creaked as they opened. Inside, Ginger rubbed the bottom of her boots on a matt and loosened her scarf. As she followed Mr. McCallum, their footsteps echoed through the entrance hall which had high vaulted ceilings and a large wooden counter area. It had obviously been put in to serve as the guest reception for the hotel. The floor was mismatched stone masonry worn in paths from arched doorway to arched doorway. The counter had recently been refinished and there was still a faint smell of linseed oil in the air. Boss sneezed twice and then wagged his stubby tail exuberantly.

"This is where we check the guests in," Mr. McCallum explained, his voice echoing off the stone walls. "Please forgive the sparseness. I've got new chairs and plants on order to make things cosier. Now, if you'll follow me, Mrs. Reed."

Ginger snapped a leash on Boss, and set him on the floor, before catching up with her long-legged host. He cast a glance over his shoulder at the sound of Boss' nails tapping on the floor.

"Is it all right?" Ginger asked.

Mr. McCallum lifted his chin. "That's fine by me."

Directly opposite the entry hall was the stair tower with stone steps rounding the corner going up on the left and down on the right. Instead of going up the stairs they entered a short, wide hallway on the right. Ginger noticed a set of swinging doors made with frosted glass that she assumed must have been newly installed.

"That's our kitchen," Mr. McCallum announced. "It was the first room I ordered to be renovated and has all the modern amenities. At the moment though, we don't have a chef, but my housekeeper, Mrs. Macleod, puts out a breakfast every morning for our guests, and keeps the tea hot."

Mr. McCallum led Ginger to the far side of the kitchen, through to a smaller, chandeliered dining area which contained a large wooden table covered in a white tablecloth and surrounded by eight wooden chairs. This opened to a sitting room where they found two men sitting in leather-upholstered armchairs near the warmth of a fireplace, sipping tea.

"Would you like a cup?" Mr. McCallum asked. Ginger thought it a great opportunity to mingle with the guests.

"Yes, that would be wonderful. Thank you"

Mr. McCallum insisted on putting a tray together, so Ginger entered the sitting room and claimed the end of a sofa, close enough to the gentlemen that she could listen in on their conversation.

However, she and Boss must've brought a welcome change of scenery as the men immediately stopped talking and stared.

"Good day," they said in unison. The man nearer to the sofa was stout and bespectacled, and looked to be in his mid-forties. Dressed in a cardigan and grey trousers, he had wispy grey hair thinning along the top. Ginger caught a whiff of cologne that smelled of citrus and sandalwood. It would actually have been a pleasing scent, if not too liberally applied.

The other man, though similar in age, was more dapper in appearance, dressed immaculately in a herringbone suit with a bow tie and coordinating pocket square handkerchief. He wore a waxed handlebar moustache, and kept his thick black hair slicked back. He wore several rings on his fingers and looked like a man out of a fashion magazine. Basil would have used the old-fashioned word "dandy" to describe him.

He smiled politely as he extended his hand, but to Ginger his eyes somehow seemed to suggest a more reluctant expression. "Douglas Grier at your service, madam."

The first man lifted a palm. "Alfred Ferguson."

As Ginger had suspected, the odorous man was the journalist Harold Macleod had mentioned.

"Mrs. Ginger Reed," Ginger said, taking a seat. "I'm a friend of Mr. McCallum's. My husband's business brought us to Edinburgh."

"A friend of the family, eh?" Mr. Grier said.

"Yes, that's right." She left it at that. She could've made up a story with far more detail, but experience in the British secret service had taught her that it was far less suspicious to give sparse detail unless specifically asked.

After commanding Boss to lie under her chair, Ginger removed her gloves and set them to the side. "Can I presume you're both guests at the castle?"

"I am not a guest here," Mr. Grier said. "I'm the owner of

the renovation company that is working on this castle."

"Oh?" Ginger was taken aback. The man's appearance did not match his chosen vocation. He seemed more likely to be in film or some other, more dramatic profession.

"Mr. McCallum has invited me here to try to convince my crew to go back to work." He chuckled dryly. "I told him it would go better if he offered some good Scotch whisky."

"I'm afraid I'm the one he has to worry about," Mr. Ferguson said. "I'm here on assignment from *The Glasgow Telegraph*. Don't be alarmed though. I'm writing a piece on the paranormal. I promise you won't be quoted on anything you may say while you are here." He winked at her. "Unless of course, you are actually an apparition yourself." He recoiled away from her slightly in mock terror. "And in that case, I would love to have a chance to interview you at some point," he said with a chuckle. His expression then grew serious. "Oh dear. I am assuming you have been told..."

Mr. McCallum entered the sitting room at that point, bringing the journalist's jesting to a close. Behind him with a tea tray was a plump woman with flat leather shoes and a faded apron over a grey wool skirt. Ginger presumed she was the groundskeeper's wife.

"I trust these gentlemen have been on their best behaviour?" Mr. McCallum said.

"Perfectly," Ginger reassured him.

Once the tea was poured, Mr. McCallum turned to his one guest. "So, Mr. Ferguson, when do you think you will be returning to Glasgow. Not that we're trying to get rid of you, but I am a wee bit curious to know what you're typing up in your room."

"Actually very soon, Mr. McCallum. I have seen more than enough to make an interesting story."

"Oh?" Ginger broke in. "What sort of things have you seen?"

A smarmy smile overtook the man's face. "Oh, I am not

going to 'reveal my sources' as we say in the newspaper business. Especially when those sources are so hard to pin down for a direct quote, eh?" Mr. Ferguson set his teacup down with a clang, and pushed away from the table as he announced, "If you'll excuse me, I need to return to my room for the afternoon."

Mr. McCallum turned to Mr. Grier. "Mrs Reed and her husband are thinking of investing in the castle."

Earlier that morning, Ginger had suggested to Mr. McCallum that this be part of her cover story. It would serve as an explanation as to why she might exhibit such a keen interest in the castle.

"I wouldn't mind if she listened in to any renovation discussions," Mr. McCallum continued, "if you don't object."

The renovation company owner shrugged his shoulders noncommittally as Mr. McCallum opened the door of a sideboard and produced a brown bottle. "A bit of Scotch with your tea?"

Mr. Grier wasn't the type to say no to freely offered spirits, it seemed, though Ginger shook her head at the offer when Mr. McCallum raised the bottle to her.

Next, Mr. McCallum presented a packet of cigars, offering Mr. Grier one. Ginger thought their host was doing everything he knew how to butter up the foreman.

The air was soon filled with bluish smoke. "So Mr. Grier," Mr. McCallum started, "let's get to it, shall we? I'm hoping your men are still around?"

"For now, yes. Staying at the Heath Inn in Blackford."

"Good. I'm quite eager to see the renovations completed. Almost half the first floor is waiting for guests, not to mention the fact that the second and third floors are not even safe to walk on right now due to crumbling ceilings and other hazards." He stared hard over the rim of his crystal glass at Mr. Grier. "But of course, that is scheduled for next year's renovations as we previously discussed. The great hall on the ground floor needs to be repainted before we can use it, and the wooden floor refinished. In addition, I would like to get electric lighting installed sometime in the not-too-distant future so preparations for that need to be put in place. Lighting by oil lamps is quaint, but not up to modern standards in the hotel industry. There is also the matter of the castle library on the ground floor. It is still waiting to have those floors refinished and the whole room repainted. All the books are currently in storage. And don't forget, I want to turn the castle dungeon into a top-rate wine cellar. Can we bolster your men enough to finish the job?"

"That will take a wee bit of bolstering all right. Especially to make them go back into that library."

"Why is that?" Ginger asked.

The two men shared a look before Mr. McCallum expanded. "As I've already mentioned, Mrs. Reed, an apparition has been seen there."

Mr. Grier poked the air with his cigar. "Twice."

"You can tell your men that I'm going to get to the bottom of this whole haunting and end it."

"Once a place is haunted, Charles, you can't just get rid of it." Mr. Grier scowled. "I wish you had told me the place was haunted *before* we started the work."

"I didn't know it was."

"Isn't that just splendid," Mr. Grier retorted. "Why don't you just contact me when the exorcism is complete."

"I've advertised nationally for a grand opening at Easter, Mr. Grier. You know that. Spring and summer are busy times for the hotel industry."

Boss whined as the men's voices grew increasingly tense. Ginger reached under her seat to give him a reassuring pat.

Mr. McCallum leaned forward, staring hard at Mr. Grier. "Tell your men that if they come back to work right away, I'm prepared to double their pay, as long as they get the job finished in the prescribed time.

A glint came into the crew boss' eyes as he regarded the offer. "You don't know if these apparitions are malicious. What if there's an injury... or even worse?" He shook his head. "No, I don't think doubling their pay will quite do it."

Mr. McCallum leaned back in his chair. "I doubt very much anything like that will happen. Ghosts, even if they are real—which they are not—are in the business of frightening people. They are supposedly caught between two dimensions, the tangible and the ethereal, and don't have any power beyond playing on people's fears. In any event, I will take full responsibility for any injuries that come to any of the men should there be doctor's expenses."

Ginger felt as if she were watching a verbal tennis match and ran her fingers along her neck which was growing stiff from turning back and forth.

Mr. Grier shrugged, seemingly unimpressed by Mr. McCallum's offer. His silence paid off, as Mr. McCallum raised the stakes.

"I'll triple the pay!"

Ginger watched Mr. Grier's response closely.

"That's a wee bit of money, Charles. Are you certain?"

"Yes, no question about it." Mr. McCallum snuffed out his cigar in the ashtray Mrs. Macleod had provided. "I can put it in writing."

Mr. Grier slowly nodded. "Very well. I'll meet with the crew in the morning and see what I can do."

Ginger guessed that the crew would be back at work very soon.

Mr. Grier made a sudden retreat, leaving Ginger and Boss alone with Mr. McCallum, though the tension remained. Ginger was beginning to regret not taking Mr. McCallum up on his offer of Scotch.

"Perhaps you could show me a bit more of the castle," Ginger said. "I'd like to see the library and the dungeon, as those two rooms seem to be frequent haunting spots."

"Of course." Mr. McCallum stood, prompting Ginger to join him.

The library was a medium-sized room on the southeast corner of the ground floor next to the stair tower and overlooking the garden where Ginger had met Mr. Macleod. The shelves were indeed empty, and one didn't need to run the tip of one's white glove along them to see that they hadn't been dusted in a while. A stone fireplace was left cold and empty, but Ginger could imagine how cosy and comfortable the room would be with a blazing fire and shelves stocked with books. There was an old wooden rolling ladder propped up against one of the shelves that would have been used at one time to access the books placed on the high shelves. The iron track that it had once rested on was nowhere to be seen.

"As you can see, there is still work to be done here," Mr. Mc Callum said wistfully.

After visiting the library, Mr. McCallum led Ginger across to the other end of the castle past the dining room and sitting room, and down a wide corridor to a large, heavy arched wooden door. As he opened it, a draught brushed Ginger's face indicating that the room beyond the door was sizeable.

"This is the meeting hall or 'great' hall as some would call it," he said, sweeping his arm around the room. "It's where banquets were held or important events such as governmental meetings and the like. The local laird would come here to show off his great wealth and influence to people outside his immediate family."

Like most castle meeting halls Ginger had seen, this one had a very high, arched wooden-beamed ceiling that made the room feel even larger. Two great arched windows let in sunlight and one could see dust motes floating in the air in the sunbeams.

"We haven't used it for anything yet, of course." Mr. McCallum's voice reverberated off of the high ceiling and stone walls. "This is waiting to be worked on," he said, pointing at the rough wooden floor that once must have been beautiful but was now in desperate need of sanding and refinishing. The floor was partially covered by a thick carpet which Ginger noticed also needed some attention.

They made their way back to the main stair tower where they then descended a few steps until they came to a heavy door which exposed a set of well-worn stone steps going even further down.

"The dungeon," Mr. McCallum explained. He lit an oil lantern—the device and a box of matches sitting on the ledge for such a purpose—and motioned for Ginger to follow. Boss sniffed each step as he kept as close as he could to Ginger's heels without tripping her.

"You mentioned a cackling sound coming from here when we first spoke," Ginger said. "Did you only hear it the one time?"

"Only once."

They reached the centre of a large stone-walled room with several chambers built into it. Quite possibly used for imprisoning people, the dungeon had a strange reverberating effect when one spoke due to the low, arched stone ceiling.

"Has anyone been down recently?" Ginger asked.

"As far as I know just myself and Mr. Grier, when I first bought the place and had him look it over and make an assessment. But that was a few months ago. At the time I heard the cackling, about a fortnight ago, I came down the next morning but could find nothing amiss."

He gestured toward one of the smaller chambers. "The plan is to restore this to its original look with new steel-bar doors to cover the entrance to these prison cells. People are always interested in castle dungeons. And doubling as a wine cellar, it's sure to be a big draw."

Ginger had to agree. But why was someone trying to sabotage Mr. McCallum's plans?

5

———

As Ginger had suspected, Basil's detective curiosity matched hers, and he was more than willing to relocate to the gloomy castle for the night.

"Perhaps we'll meet the ghosts of Christmas past, present, and future," he said with mirth as he drove their hired motorcar to the main entry and switched off the engine.

"I do hope to run into *something*," Ginger said. Or more to the point, some*one*.

Charles McCallum was waiting for them at the registration desk when they arrived.

"Even though you are here working on my behalf, I do hope you will find your stay at Kirksbridge Castle to be pleasant."

Mr. McCallum wrote their names in the ledger as if they were paying guests and assigned them a room.

"It's the best we have available at the moment," he said as he retrieved a set of iron keys from the wall behind him and passed them to Basil. "I'm sorry to report that our kitchen is closed for the evening, though if you need something, drinks or a sandwich, I can look for Mrs. Macleod."

"We ate before we came," Ginger said. "But I wouldn't mind coffee. Perhaps a flask?"

Mr. McCallum grinned. "Planning on staying up for a spirit watch, are you?"

"It's what I'm here for."

"I'll have it delivered to your room."

"That's perfect, thank you."

Mr. McCallum's eyes landed on the two suitcases at Basil's feet and a frown tugged at his lips. "Would you like me to carry your luggage for you? I'm afraid I've yet to engage a porter."

The man's lack of enthusiasm made it easy for Basil to answer. "I can manage well enough."

Ginger had her make-up and jewellery kit in one hand and her handbag in the other. Boss followed them on foot.

Looking relieved, Mr. McCallum said, "Your room is on the first floor." They followed the man up the spiralling stone stair tower and down a short corridor, stopping at a door, second on the right.

Basil had to work the key before the mechanisms inside clicked and the lock was released. He chuckled. "I wonder if it's the ghost holding the handle from the other side, not wanting us to go in for some reason."

Ginger laughed along with him, though she wondered if perhaps her brave husband was a little unnerved by the possibility of a paranormal encounter.

The room had been tastefully decorated with new red and sea-foam-green paisley wallpaper trimmed with carved moulding, freshly painted white. It had its own water closet with modern plumbing and a generous wooden wardrobe.

The view out of the window was a winter wonderland. The fog had lifted allowing for a panoramic view of the craggy landscape and nearby forests.

"I can see why this would make a wonderful holiday spot."

"Shall we take a look about?" Basil asked. Ginger had had

the privilege of touring the castle, but Basil was yet to have his curiosity satisfied.

"Yes, we must," Ginger said. She searched for Boss, but the little dog had already curled up in the middle of the bed, his eyes closed and a soft snore emitting from his little black nose.

Ginger smiled. "I'm afraid he's worn out."

"He'll be fine if we leave him behind."

Basil's statement almost sounded like a question and Ginger had to hold in a grin. "Quite. He's already had a castle tour, and if a ghost does decide to make an appearance, I'm certain Boss will be delighted by the diversion.

In usual circumstances, Ginger wouldn't be tempted to try the handles on the closed doors in the corridor, but she was on the premises to sniff out a ghoul, so she made it a point to check each one. However, door after door proved to be locked.

"Oh, blast it!"

"I believe ghosts can move through locked doors," Basil said.

"Sadly, I cannot." Ginger had her gloved hand on the last door when it clicked open. "Aha."

Her delight was short-lived as the room was unfinished and in disarray, clearly waiting its turn for Mr. Grier's men to work their magic and renovate it for future use.

"It's probable that all the locked doors have a similar situation behind them," Ginger said.

"Your client would be happy to open them at your request I would think."

"Perhaps in the morning."

Ginger led Basil down the stairs and showed him the library, regaling him with the story of the apparitions that had appeared inside. From there she showed him the sitting room, the kitchen, and finally they approached the door to the dungeon.

"Drat!" Ginger said. "It's locked."

Basil loosened his tie. "I think I'd prefer to see the dungeon in the light of day."

Ginger smiled. "There's not light of day down there, love. Pitch black, no matter the time." She motioned to the cubby hole where the gas lantern and matches had been then stilled. They were gone. Mr. McCallum must've forgotten to return them.

As they passed the sitting room for the second time, they bumped into Mr. Ferguson dressed in his dinner jacket.

"Mr. Ferguson, good evening," Ginger said. "Do you remember me from earlier on?"

"Yes, of course. How could I forget such a beautiful lady? Where is your little dog?"

"He's asleep in our room. This is my husband, Basil Reed. We're guests in the hotel tonight as well. Basil, this is Mr. Ferguson."

The two men exchanged a handshake.

"I was about to smoke a cigarette and help myself to McCallum's Scotch. Would you like to join me?"

"We'd be delighted," Ginger said.

In the sitting room, Basil paused to stoke the fire as Ginger lowered herself onto one end of the sofa. Mr. Ferguson made himself at home with Mr. McCallum's Scotch, pouring two glasses. Ginger held the slight she felt at the man's presumption that she'd not be interested in a glass, but it was better that she kept a clear head.

Once they were seated, Mr. Ferguson lit a cigarette then offered one to Basil. Basil glanced at Ginger with a look that said he was only accepting to make the man comfortable. Though he smoked on occasion, it hadn't become habitual.

"Are you enjoying your stay, Mr. Ferguson?" Ginger asked.

He snorted. "I'll be honest. I feel a little less uneasy knowing I'm not the only guest sleeping here tonight."

Ginger cocked her head. "Do you believe there really is a ghost haunting this castle?"

Mr. Ferguson blew out a plume of smoke, then sipped his Scotch. He finally answered by saying, "It's all a wee bit hard to believe, isn't it?"

"Is it?" Ginger asked. "You must believe something, otherwise, why stay this long?"

"Well, I have heard things." He shifted his weight and leaned towards her. "The housekeeper, Mrs. Macleod, has confided in me. She's had objects go missing or move from one place to another. Books, lamps, keys... things like that." He glanced about the room as if to ensure no one else had entered, then lowered his voice even more until it was just above a whisper. "But I think there's an even better story going on here than just an ordinary wandering spirit."

"Oh?" Basil said. "Not something criminal?"

"I can't really say, sir. But it turns out, the Macleods have a wee bit of history with Gilbert McCallum, Charles McCallum's great uncle. I don't think Charles even knows about it."

"Oh, how interesting." Ginger crossed her legs and placed a fist under her chin, showing extreme interest, hoping it would spur the journalist to keep talking.

"Mary Macleod's father, Angus Dougal, was employed by Gilbert McCallum as a groundskeeper. He sought to borrow money from the senior McCallum to invest in a small business in a town nearby. He saw it as a way to improve his standing in life, being a partner in a printing shop, you see. Anyway, Gilbert McCallum initially agreed to help him invest but when he actually saw the business plan, he reneged on his agreement. A bit of a rotten thing to do, I would say. Angus Dougal died of a heart attack the next day."

"How dreadful!" Ginger said. Any death was a sad affair, but she didn't quite get the connection. She stared at Mr. Ferguson with wide eyes, willing him to continue. After another slow sip of his Scotch, he did.

"It happened just at the beginning of the war, madam. Charles was serving in France and I doubt very much he even knows about it. Gilbert McCallum took that wee bit of history to his grave with him as a secret, I'll wager. I discovered this by interviewing people in the surrounding villages who were around at that time."

"Soo..." Ginger thought she would let the journalist finish stating his theory.

"I believe the whole ghost story is a sham designed to thwart the McCallums' plans for this property. I will bet my last farthing that when they give up on the whole plan, the ghostings will stop."

6
———

When Ginger and Basil returned to their room, the coffee Ginger had requested was sitting on a tray on the floor of the corridor outside their door.

Basil pulled a face. "It'll be lukewarm."

"I don't mind," Ginger said. She'd consumed terrible coffee substitutes during the war and now anything "real" tasted fine to her.

Basil offered to stay awake to keep her company, but he did have a lecture to give the next day, so when his resolve was overtaken by snoring, Ginger let him sleep. She had a book to keep her company, and Boss.

Ginger let out a sigh as she sat in the chair and put her feet up on the footstool. Perhaps nothing would happen tonight except a relaxing night of T.S. Eliot and perhaps a bit of Marcel Proust if she could stay awake long enough. She had enough wood to keep the fire going all night and felt toasty warm even as the wind whistled through the windows.

Ginger was near to calling it quits as her chin kept lowering to her chest but was startled awake at two in the morning when Boss suddenly jumped up and ran to the door. He stared at the door handle intently, emitting a low growl.

"What's the matter, Bossy?" Ginger whispered as she went over to the door and cautiously opened it. She strained her ears. There was not so much as a creaking floorboard since the castle floor and walls were made of thick stone; just the wind occasionally sighing through the windows.

Then suddenly, a woman's voice could be heard moaning loudly from somewhere down below, her voice echoing off the stone walls of the nearby stair tower which seemed to almost amplify the sound. The voice rose in intensity to resemble a cry of grief, as if someone was lamenting over the sudden loss of a loved one.

Ginger spoke to Boss. "That's our cue."

Using a match, she lit one of the oil lamps from the bedside table and stepped out into the corridor, Boss at her heels.

Mr. Ferguson, the only other guest on the floor, seemed to have not yet been bothered by the noise and the corridor was quiet. As the lamp cast dancing shadows on the walls, she slowly made her way to the stair tower.

Stepping cautiously down the stairs, Ginger reached the ground floor, but the moment her foot touched the stone floor of the grand lobby, the noises stopped. She stilled, holding her lamp out high in front of her. Boss sat on his haunches staring at her curiously.

"Stay alert," she whispered to him.

Ginger slowly made her way to the kitchen, through the dining area, then back into the entrance foyer where she noticed one of the doors leading off of the main entry hall had been cracked open. Funny. Ginger didn't remember seeing what was behind that door as Mr. McCallum had failed to show her. She pressed her fingers against the door, and it swung open, not a creak to be heard. Clearly, it had been recently oiled.

The light of Ginger's lamp revealed a small, musty-smelling storage room, almost completely empty except for a few bags of flour and some tinned food. If the noise had originated here, the source was now gone. Puzzled, Ginger headed back to the lobby only to hear what sounded like a large chain being dragged across a wooden floor coming from the direction of the library.

As she approached the closed door of the library, her nose twitched at a pungent odour, like a strange mixture of wormwood and smoke.

The scent increased in intensity as she came to the library. She opened the door, entered the room, and as she stood there, a strange prickling sensation ran down her spine. Boss let out a low growl as Ginger peered about the room by the light of her lamp. A mist formed along the floor reaching knee level, as if the fog had come indoors.

Out of nowhere, the luminescent figure of a woman dressed in a ragged evening dress suddenly appeared. Her bedraggled hair partially obscured her face as she silently wept.

Oh mercy.

The image was translucent, the empty row of bookshelves behind it shimmering through it, as if the crying figure were made of vapour. The spectre dropped her hands and stretched them out towards Ginger as if imploring her to help, revealing a horrible scar on her left cheek.

Ginger's heart jumped to her throat as the strange figure disappeared as abruptly as it had appeared. She glanced down at Boss who was almost totally obscured by the strange fog.

"Bossy? Didn't you see that?" She could just make out his pug nose and two eyes looking up questioningly at her through the mist. How strange that he hadn't even growled or barked, instead he sneezed and then licked his chops.

"I guess not."

The mist had obscured the dog's eyesight. Sometimes it wasn't easy being seventeen inches tall.

In a flash, the mysterious figure appeared again in the

very same spot. Ginger recoiled from the sight but bravely fought the urge to turn and run. This time the woman opened her mouth as if to let out a shriek but, as before, no sound was emitted. At the same time, the piercing sound of a woman wailing reached them from outside the library, and this time Boss barked furiously. Ginger's attention shot to the open door, and when she looked back the apparition was gone.

She ran out of the room into the foyer.

"Who's there?" she called out. "Is everyone all right?"

"What the devil is going on?"

Charles McCallum stepped into view, wrapping the belt of his housecoat around his waist. "Was it the spirit? She's certainly making a fuss tonight, isn't she?"

Could a ghost be in two places at once?

The woman's voice sounded like it was now coming from the meeting hall at the east end of the ground floor. Ginger rushed toward the wailing with Boss at her heels and Mr. McCallum racing ahead. As soon as he pushed the door open and they stepped into the large room, the sound stopped.

"Don't let her get away!" Mr. Ferguson stumbled into the room. "I heard the commotion. Did you see her? Did you see the spirit of Lady McBain?"

"Is there another entrance to this room, Mr. McCallum? Perhaps a hidden door?"

Mr. McCallum ran fingers through his messy hair. "No, not that I know of."

After an awkward moment of the three of them staring at each other, Ginger said, "Let's go to the library. The apparition was there only a moment ago."

They stood for another moment or two before Ginger again suggested they all go to the library. As she suspected, the mist was now completely gone.

"Nothing seems out of the ordinary here," Mr. McCallum said.

Ginger let out a defeated sigh. "I doubt it will come back now."

"Why do you say that?" asked Mr. Ferguson. "Do you have experience with ghosts?"

"Not really," Ginger replied. "But I have a lot of experience with deception." She let her gaze linger on the man's face. "Gentlemen, if you'll excuse me. I'm feeling rather tired after all this excitement. I'll see you in the morning."

With that, Ginger left the room, Boss trotting resolutely beside her.

7

———

*A*s Ginger and Basil enjoyed an adequate breakfast put together by Mrs. Macleod—Boss accepting scraps of bacon in exchange for his good behaviour—Ginger relayed the excitement of the night before.

"And to think I missed all of that!" Basil said. He poked at his boiled egg forlornly. "I suppose it would be too much to ask you to wait until my session is over this afternoon so that I might join in with the fun."

"I'll do my best, love."

It was a promise Ginger had to give up on before she had finished her cup of tea. As Basil left for his seminar, Ginger's mind went back to the meeting hall and the wailing she'd heard coming from there in the middle of the night. Perhaps she'd have another quick look. Her intention was thwarted by the door being closed and locked, and when she searched for either of the Macleods or Mr. McCallum, she found she was quite alone in the castle, at least on the ground floor.

Not one to be bested by a locked door, Ginger retrieved a set of lock picks from her handbag. Not a usual item for a lady to carry about with her, but Ginger wasn't usual and her handbag contained a number of items another person might raise an eyebrow over.

After jimmying with the picks, the lock mechanism finally clicked open. Instinctively, Ginger glanced about her, and once assured that her transgression was unwitnessed, she and Boss slipped inside.

Mr. McCallum had insisted that there wasn't a second exit to the meeting hall, but even due to the size, that statement felt false. However, a rudimentary scan of the room didn't produce signs of an alternate way out. Ginger brushed the cold stone walls with the palms of her hands.

"I promise you there is no hidden door in those walls."

Ginger turned at the sound of Mr. McCallum's voice.

"Oh, hello," she said. "Please forgive my curiosity."

"Not at all. It's why I hired you, Mrs. Reed. But you must know that I've consulted the castle plans, examining every bit of the structure, and a secret passageway wasn't found anywhere."

"Castles that are hundreds of years old have drawings that are known to be very inaccurate," Ginger said as she kept walking, one hand tracing the wall. "Besides, it wouldn't be a secret passage if its presence wasn't kept a secret. Especially in a drawing."

Mr. McCallum conceded. "I suppose that's true."

Ginger came to the end of the last wall and stood for a moment feeling a bit puzzled as she dusted off her hands.

Boss, sniffing at the myriad of smells coming from the thick carpet that covered most of the floor, looked up at Ginger and let out a short bark.

"It's okay, Boss, we'll find it."

Boss whined and pawed at the carpet.

"Boss! Don't do that," Ginger scolded. "You'll ruin it."

"This old carpet is not worth two farthings," Mr. McCallum said. "We'll throw it out when the floors are renovated."

Ginger thought for a moment. "Have you ever removed the carpet?"

Mr. McCallum looked at her for a few seconds before answering. "No... I mean, not yet..." he stopped mid-sentence as a sudden thought came to him.

"Would you?" Ginger asked as she walked to the edge of the carpet and bent down.

"Yes, of course." Ginger and Mr. McCallum bent over and rolled up the carpet. It was heavy and musty but not hard to handle. Boss jumped out of the way as a wooden trapdoor, built flush with the surface, came into view.

Ginger dusted off her hands again by clapping them together. "Good job, Bossy!"

It took only a moment to pry the door open. It was rather heavy, but the hinges offered no squeaks or groans and looked like they had been recently replaced. Beneath the opening was a set of ancient stone steps. "I wonder where these go," Ginger muttered.

"I'll go and get a lantern," Mr. McCallum offered.

"That's not necessary," Ginger said. "I have a torch in my handbag."

As they started down, Ginger kept her fingers along the jagged stone wall to aid her balance as the steps grew continually narrower and steeper. An unlit lantern hung from a hook at the foot of the steps, and Ginger placed a palm on it, finding it cool to the touch.

"It hasn't been lit recently," Ginger commented. "But it's dust free. Someone used it not long ago."

They found an entrance to a tunnel at the bottom of the steps. It had an arch about the height of a tall man, and so it was relatively easy to quickly navigate through the passage. They soon came to a fork in the tunnel; one kept going straight ahead to the right and the other was a narrow stone staircase leading up and to the left. They decided to follow the right one which eventually led them to a thick wooden door that was locked from the other side. Ginger looked enquiringly at Mr. McCallum who shrugged.

A dead end for now.

Returning to the fork, they headed down the alternate route for some distance until they were stopped by another door at the top of a small flight of steps. Ginger gave it a shove and it swung open.

They found themselves standing in a windowless room about eight feet square with some very odd items stored in it. The largest of these was a six-by-four-foot sheet of glass hanging from a steel clothing rack on wheels, the kind one normally would expect to see backstage at a theatre. The outside edges of the glass were covered in a black felt, and it was affixed to the rack with black chains. There were also two Atlas brand car batteries sitting on the stone floor, one wired to a small theatrical floor spotlight and the other to an electrical floor fan. The area reminded Ginger of a backstage props room in a theatre.

The walls had all been painted black. In addition, there were several glass jars next to the fan and some very large, short candles with multiple wicks in each of them. Two of the large jars were labelled *glycerine* and three more were labelled *distilled water*. There was also a large steel ring stand and crucible, the kind one might see for heating liquids in a laboratory. On a small wooden shelf was a rumpled pile of clothing, and a small case of theatrical make-up. Ginger picked up the clothes and unrolled them. Tunics, white and tattered.

Perfect costumes for a tormented ghost.

"What is all this?" Mr. McCallum asked, looking around the room.

"You might as well name the ghost 'Mrs. Pepper'," Ginger said.

"I don't understand."

Ignoring the comment, Ginger held up her lamp and walked over to the opposite wall where a doorknob jutted out of the middle of it at about waist height. On closer inspection she found the seam of a door. Turning the knob, Ginger pushed, but it was as solid as a brick wall, and did not give way. She stepped back momentarily frustrated. She then turned the handle again and pulled. The door swung inwards without effort. When she stepped through, she was amazed to find herself in the library. The door had been built with a bookcase attached to the front of it as a deception. Walking to the opposite side of the room, she saw that with the hidden door swung open, the library was actually an L-shaped chamber. Ginger stood where the ghost had been standing when she'd seen it, directly across from the hidden door.

Clever.

Suddenly, a single bark could be heard from the hall below them. Ginger and Mr. McCallum rushed down the stairs and into the corridor to find Mr. Ferguson staring down the hatch to the passageway below.

Boss continued to bark, as he announced the arrival of Mr. Ferguson, who joined them from the ground-floor doorway. He trotted to the bookshelf sitting out of place to see the hidden room behind it.

"A secret passage!" He turned to Ginger and Mr. McCallum. "I'm frightfully glad I stayed here long enough to see *this!*"

"Indeed," Ginger said. This was the second time Mr. Ferguson had appeared just as a new discovery was made. How convenient.

"Mr. McCallum," Ginger started. "Are the workmen to arrive today?"

"Mr. Grier telephoned me this morning with good news. Work on the renovation begins again tomorrow!"

Ginger was thrilled for her client, but she was quite certain there was someone close by who wasn't.

"Mr. McCallum, if you wouldn't mind, I'd like to take another look at the dungeon."

. . .

BACK IN THE belly of the castle, Ginger ran the beam of her torch along the walls. Her eye was drawn to the stonework of the second chamber where some of the mortar appeared thin and rather newer than the surrounding bricks.

Retrieving a pencil from her handbag, Ginger scratched at a portion of the mortar—one mustn't ruin one's manicure if not necessary—and it came away like wet soil.

Fake.

She dug the pencil with some force into the crumbling mortar and immediately the brick came loose. She glanced at Mr. McCallum. "There's wood underneath."

Mr. McCallum, whose face showed a mixture of fear and bafflement, helped to clear away the remainder of the poorly assembled wall structure. Behind it was a thick wooden door.

It opened easily with a loud creak to reveal yet another dark, musty-smelling chamber.

"It smells like the dead!"

"The dead smell much worse than this," Ginger said. She stepped further into the small chamber. "It looks to me like this was part of the prison chamber. Perhaps it was meant for groups of prisoners to be held, and a wall with a door was built to partition it long ago. This false wall was built recently to hide that fact."

"But why?"

Ginger aimed her torch towards the far wall. Leaning against it, supported by beams of wood to keep them off the floor, were several groups of large, flat objects covered in clean cloth.

Ginger firmly grasped the cloth covering the first one, threw it off, and shone her torch on a wooden-framed oil painting of two couples sitting at a street cafe. The two women were dressed in bright, white Victorian-era dresses while the men wore dinner jackets from the same era.

"Looks like a *Charpentier*," said Mr. McCallum. Ginger stared at him in surprise. He added, "If that's an original it is worth thousands."

Was the man an art expert?

Ginger uncovered a few more of the paintings. If they were originals, they were indeed worth a fortune, and quite likely were stolen. Mr. McCallum stood there as if dumbstruck.

"You must lock the door to this dungeon and not breathe a word of it to anyone," Ginger said. "The positive solution to this case depends highly upon it."

"Not a word," he repeated.

"Good. I will be back by seven."

As she stepped into the main chamber, she noticed Boss chewing on what looked like some sort of cloth toy. "What have you got there?" She bent down to examine it as Boss looked on, keeping his eyes locked on the object as she lifted it. It was a stained red handkerchief.

8

Ginger and Basil, with Boss trotting alongside them, entered the castle sitting room at precisely 7 p.m. There was a crackling fire in the fireplace, and the assembly Ginger had requested was seated around the tea table wearing various mixed expressions of displeasure and nervousness. Along with Mr. McCallum were Mr. and Mrs. Macleod, Douglas Grier, and Alfred Ferguson who pulled hard on a lit cigar and released the fragrant plume of smoke into the room. They stared at Ginger and Basil who stood by the doorway.

"What the dickens is this all about, McCallum?" Mr. Grier said. "I've got a bloody lot of work to do as you well know."

Charles McCallum raised a brow in Ginger's direction.

"If you would allow me," Ginger said, "I can explain. But first, for those of you who've yet to meet my husband, let me introduce Chief Inspector Basil Reed of Scotland Yard."

Mrs. Macleod jerked backwards. "Scotland Yard!"

Alfred Ferguson shot Basil a look of suspicion then pointed the glowing end of his cigar at Ginger. "Please do get on with it. I, for one, have a deadline to meet."

Basil took the floor. "I came to Edinburgh as a training consultant for the Edinburgh police. My presence here is somewhat incidental. I *would* like however, to introduce you to my wife."

"We've already—" started Mr. Grier.

"If I may," Basil interrupted, "Mrs Ginger Reed, otherwise known as Lady Gold from the office of Lady Gold Investigations, Watson Street, London."

"Can we dispense with the riddles?" Mr. Ferguson said.

"No riddles, my good sir," Mr. McCallum replied. "I hired Mrs. Reed, known also as Lady Gold, to investigate the ghostings."

Mr. Grier laughed. "And did she meet one during her stay?"

"As it stands," Ginger answered, "yes and no."

"Again," Mr. Ferguson grumbled. "More riddles."

Ginger strolled to the fireplace where she could be seen clearly by all in the room. "As Mr. McCallum has already stated, I'm here to get to the bottom of this whole ghost business which has very inconveniently been delaying his renovation plans."

Mr. McCallum's chin jutted into the air, as if to underscore his perceived injury.

Ginger continued, "However, I was quite surprised to find a newspaper man here. Why would a man concerned about a bad reputation from a haunting, tolerate a journalist from *The Glasgow Telegraph* when he knew that journalist was writing a story about it?"

"Now, look here..." Mr. McCallum began.

"It would make the place far more famous, that's why," Mr. Ferguson blustered. "That much is obvious. Thrill seekers would flock to this place from all over Britain. There are many who would pay top money for the chance to see a real ghost!"

"And what a coup for you, Mr. Ferguson. You haven't exactly had any big stories in the last few years, have you?"

"I am not sure what you are getting at."

"You told me that ghost stories are commonplace these days in *The Glasgow Telegraph*. Yet, when I spoke to your chief editor today on the telephone, he said they hadn't had a ghost story for a very long time. After a bit of prodding, he also told me that if you didn't deliver a good story soon, your position with them would be in peril. But you already knew that, didn't you, Mr. Ferguson?"

The journalist narrowed his eyes, his jaw clenching, ignoring the ashes from his cigar that fell to the floor.

Ginger pushed a lock of her red hair behind one ear. "Your research regarding Harold and Mary Macleod was correct though. I checked with city and bank records." Turning to the couple, she added, "For all of your complaints about the ghostings, you have no objection to one, do you?"

Mr. and Mrs. Macleod's eyes had long lost their friendly gleam.

"I suspect your employment here had only one purpose," Ginger said, "to witness first-hand the demise of Mr. McCallum's dream of turning this castle into a hotel. Isn't that why you stayed when the rest of the staff left? I believe you signed up for employment here in order to sabotage the enterprise, but when the ghost appeared, you were happy to let it do the job for you."

Mr. McCallum huffed. "Why on earth would they do that?"

"It's an interesting, but sad story, Mr. McCallum." She nodded towards Mr. Ferguson, who stabbed at the ashtray, putting out his cigar. "I am sure your journalist friend would be happy to fill you in on it later."

"And now we come to Mr. Grier." Ginger gestured towards the crew boss who had been rather quiet thus far. He raised an eyebrow at the mention of his name.

"But of course," he said with a smirk. "Why should I think

I could escape this ridiculous escapade. Please do continue, *Lady Gold*."

"It wouldn't be the first time that a crew of renovation workers has sought to extort larger fees from a customer by creating a false challenge. A ghosting is quite a clever ruse."

The crew boss sneered as the sentence hung in the air.

Ginger noticed Basil watching her with a boyish grin on his face and held his gaze.

You're enjoying this, aren't you, Mr. Reed?

Taking a breath, she faced the group. "All of this leads me to my main point. You see, there's of course the matter of the stolen artwork."

Jaws slackened around the circle.

"I admit to being puzzled by a few things. The first is that you, Mr. McCallum, could so readily identify the *Charpentier* original."

Mr. McCallum sat tall. "I studied art at Edinburgh University. I was terrible at it and only lasted a year, but there you have it. Anyway, *Charpentier* was famous for his cafe scenes."

"I see." Ginger nodded. "The second thing is this." From her handbag she pulled a red handkerchief. "My sweet dog, Boss, came across this in the dungeon. Care to explain, Mr. Macleod, since you told me you had never, and would never, go down there?"

The man's face turned as red as the cloth itself. "I... well, I went down there last night. With all this ghost talk, well I... I guess curiosity got the better of me."

"Liar!"

The growl came from Mr. Grier, who stared at Mr. Macleod with such a malicious glare that Ginger was glad the men sat out of arm's reach of each other.

"Do you have something to add, Mr. Grier?" Ginger asked. She held his gaze. "Or should I say, *Mr. Leeds*. At least, that's the name you used when you signed out the book on castle history at the library a month ago. The same one I read just yesterday morning." Mr Grier shot her an angry look. "Yes, the librarian was nice enough to give me your description today. You and I are the only ones in over a year to read that book. Curious isn't it? Did you enjoy the story about the noble woman who was attacked with pruning shears?"

"Mr. Grier, rather, Mr. Leeds...." Ginger tilted her head. "Or I could call you *Mephisto,* isn't that right?"

"Of course!" Mr. Ferguson shouted. "I *knew* I had seen you before." He pointed a finger across the room. "Bloody hell!"

"Please enlighten us, Mr. Ferguson," Ginger offered.

"*Mephisto,* illusionist... magician... stage actor. I saw your show once in Glasgow years ago. You made a lady disappear off the stage!" He looked excitedly around the room. "This man is a genius. The show was spell binding!"

"Interesting words to describe it. *Spells* and the like," Ginger remarked. "But not as lucrative as selling stolen art, is it, Mr. Mephisto? And if you *are* a genius, I wonder about the wisdom of posing as a crew boss in a renovation crew. Do you know that the Glasgow police have a warrant out for the arrest of a suspected dealer in stolen art? A man who fits your description? A man they have suspected for years is the very same man as Mephisto, the famous magician, but have been unable to prove? A man who collects art from thieves, hides it until the police have all but given up looking for it and then sells it to unscrupulous collectors all across Europe. I imagine it's not easy to find a safe spot for all that artwork. A dungeon in an abandoned castle might be a good place."

Ginger squeezed Basil's shoulder as she walked behind him. "The Edinburgh police were quite helpful with their records today, weren't they, dear? It seems there're quite a few unsolved cases of stolen art in Scotland. Who would have thought?"

Mr. Mephisto flicked his fingers into the air. "This is a fairy tale, no more real than this ghost."

"Is it?" Ginger said. "I agree that the ruse would be too much for one man, even a genius like you, Mr. Mephisto. Especially when one must conjure up a ghost to keep guests and staff to a minimum until the artwork could be retrieved and sold off. It takes a crew really.

"Someone to let you into a locked castle at night perhaps." Ginger gestured towards Mr. Macleod who sneered across the room at Mr. Grier, his strange, canines in full view. "Perhaps in return for a percentage of the sales, that person could also show you all the hidden passageways and doors that this castle offers. At any rate, it takes more than one person to rattle chains and thump on the wall in one room, while shrieking like a tormented lady in another room. Or, as in my experience, when a ghost appears in one room, but the sound of her lament is heard down below. Because of this, I failed to inspect the library as closely as I most assuredly would have done had the noise not drawn me away. Very clever indeed."

"But how? How was it done?" Mr. Ferguson asked. "The apparition, the strange smells?"

"Care to explain, Mr. Mephisto?"

"Magicians don't reveal their secrets," the man growled.

"Then allow me," Ginger said. "It's called Pepper's Illusion after the man who invented it. Henry Pepper to be exact. As an investigator intrigued by the art of deception, I found *The History of Illusion* to be a very interesting read indeed. The illusion involves a sheet of glass placed at a forty-five-degree angle to refract a spotlight shining on an actor dressed in women's clothing and stage make-up. An L-shaped chamber is needed to create the illusion, so it's convenient that the library has a hidden chamber, isn't it?"

"And the smells? The mists?" Mr. McCallum asked.

"The glycerine, distilled water, and a low-running electrical fan we found in the hidden chamber off the library can account for that. A heated-up mixture creates a low-lying fog. The scents are easy to obtain from any perfume shop, and one just adds them to the mixture of water and glycerine."

Mr. McCallum sat forward, elbows on his knees. "So that evil cackling I heard coming from the dungeon...."

"The scraping and digging noises you heard came from the effort of moving artwork. They heard you coming and scared you off."

"Charlatan!" Mr. McCallum pointed an accusing finger at the illusionist.

"Indeed, he is," Ginger said. "But then... *all* of you have been less than forthright, isn't that true? Mr. McCallum claimed to fear a loss of reputation and yet allowed Mr. Ferguson, who also lied about the real story he was writing, to stay here. Hiring me, I would wager, just added to the story. The Macleods lied about their reason for being employed at the castle *and* were accessories to a crime. Mr. Mephisto may be an art thief, but he's not the only charlatan in this room."

A defiant silence loomed, until four uniformed constables, whom Basil had summoned earlier, entered the room.

9

____

Ginger and Basil had returned to *The Baron's Hotel* and the next morning enjoyed a lovely Scottish break-fast of sausages and eggs, black pudding, sautéed mushrooms, and half a tomato. Christmas music played on a gramophone in the corner and through the windows, snow could be seen falling softly, deadening the sounds of motor buses and the bells of horse-drawn carts.

"I think you should come with me to the lectures today and give a talk on detective dramatics," Basil said, a wry smile on his lips as he lifted his coffee cup. "That was quite a meeting you conducted last night. Like something out of a novel."

"I thank you," Ginger said sweetly, "but no. There are still dress shops in this city that need my inspection, and I want to do a little Christmas shopping while I'm here."

Ginger's mind went to Hartigan House in South Kensington, where she and Basil lived with Ginger's grandmother, Ambrosia, the Dowager Lady Gold, her sister-in-law, Felicia Gold, and her young ward, Scout. As much as Ginger was ready for some time away, she felt her heart twinge with longing to return to her family.

She focused back on her husband's comments. "As for the meeting," she said, "you know I'm not one for theatrics, but I'm afraid it couldn't be avoided. After we found the paintings, I had my suspicions, but I needed proof. I'd gathered enough information on Mr. Mephisto yesterday afternoon, but I still suspected that the Macleods were involved."

Basil tapped his chin. "The red handkerchief."

"Exactly." Ginger reached down to slip Boss a piece of sausage, not to forget the dog's part in the discovery. "I hoped my presentation would bring the truth out."

"And it did. Although Mephisto remains uncooperative, some of his cohorts are not. The police tell me they had a full confession last night from two of them. They claim Mephisto had moved all the artwork into the castle months before McCallum decided to move in and renovate. Mephisto hadn't expected that, so he had to come up with something to keep the castle inhabitants to a minimum. He approached McCallum immediately and offered to renovate at a low price so that he could make sure McCallum hired him and his men."

"Not actually workmen," Ginger guessed.

"Well, a few of them have had some renovation experience, which explains why the castle's renovations were successful. But generally speaking, no they weren't really workmen, but rather a ring of thieves led by Mephisto. Macleod happened upon them one night, just as you suspected, so they cut him in on a small portion of the profits to gain his cooperation." Basil paused and then added. "Well, I guess the Edinburgh police won't need me to consult on those stolen art thefts anymore. I shall have to come up with something else for Thursday."

"You'll think of something, love." Ginger placed her hand on her husband's arm. "I'm glad it's all over now. In truth," her voice took on the lilt of teasing, "I'm surprised that an accomplished detective like you hasn't worked it out already."

"Oh? And what is that?"

"I love shopping, Mr. Reed. When there's a whole city full of unexplored dress shops, hat shops, and shoe boutiques, there isn't the 'ghost' of a chance I will be deterred."

THE END.

THE CASE OF THE MISSING CHRISTMAS GOOSE

1

———

*M*rs. Ginger Reed, professionally known as Lady Gold, was having tea with her younger sister-in-law, Miss Felicia Gold, in the sitting room at Hartigan House, Ginger's large sandstone property in South Kensington. It was a cold, wintry day—wisps of snow fell outside the tall windows facing the street, the wrought-iron fencing silver with ice—and Ginger was grateful for the warm crackling fire in the stone fireplace. *The Mermaid* from a Waterhouse painting hanging above the mantel, watched intently. Boss, Ginger's beloved Boston terrier, snored on the Persian carpet, stretched out just near Ginger's feet where she sat in one of the velvet wingback chairs. For fun, Ginger would poke him with her toes just to hear him grunt and roll over onto his other side which made Felicia giggle.

"I can't believe Basil had to go to work today," Felicia remarked, her eyes wide with indignation. Basil Reed, Ginger's husband, was a chief inspector at Scotland Yard, and his work kept him busy as a matter of course.

"It is almost Christmas after all," Felicia continued, pouting. Her pretty heart-shaped face never failed to fondly remind Ginger of her first husband, Daniel, Lord Gold, who had died in the Great War. *His* temperament had been far different from his younger sister's. Daniel had been a man with good humour, but it was tempered with a high sense of propriety, something his more impetuous sibling seemed to lack at times. Still, the two ladies had grown very close, and continued to be so, even after Ginger had married Basil. One in Felicia's social class could easily grow bored and dip one's toes in scandal, but Ginger had reined her sister-in-law in with a promise of intrigue whilst working in the office of *Lady Gold Investigations* where they were employed by private individuals for investigative work.

"Christmas Eve isn't until tomorrow," Ginger replied. "Besides, criminals don't look at their watches and pause their nefarious acts for teatime; well at least the worst of them don't. Nor do they look at their calendars and decide not to rob a bank just because Father Christmas may soon arrive and they don't want to get into his bad books." She raised her ginger eyebrows at Felicia who couldn't help giving a small smile at the teasing remark.

"*You* didn't go into your investigative office today," Felicia said, jutting out her chin.

Ginger blew on her hot tea, took a sip, then said, "I don't have a police force to manage."

"You didn't even go to *Feathers & Flair*."

Ginger's Regent Street boutique dress shop had gained quite a reputation in a short amount of time for fine imported high-fashion frocks, hats, and accessories.

"I have very able staff, as you know." Ginger waved fingers towards the windows. "Besides, who is going to go outside in that weather today to buy a hat?" Both women glanced outside at the blowing snow. Winter had definitely decided to tip its hat and say hello to London today.

Lizzie Weaver came into the room with a plate of fragrant freshly made mince pies, putting the decorative plate on the table. "Mrs. Beasley has baked mince pies." Though her eyes were averted, Ginger noticed their puffiness. The young maid sniffed, then said, "Would you like anything else, madam?"

"I think we're fine here, Lizzie, thank you, but is something wrong?" Ginger asked. "You look rather down for such a joyous time of year."

Lizzie wrung her hands, clasped low and pressing against her apron. Under her white maid's cap, her face bloomed a deep red, as if the question had taken her by surprise. "Oh no, madam. I'm fine. So sorry...I." She nodded awkwardly. "If there's nothing else."

"That is all, thank you."

The maid curtsied and quickly left the room. Ginger shot a concerned look at Felicia who shrugged a thin shoulder. Something was definitely going on with Lizzie, but Ginger didn't want to pry.

Ginger reached for a mince pie. "I can't wait to see your reaction to what I've bought you for Christmas..."

Felicia's eyes widened and she opened her mouth to reply, but was cut off by the sound of crashing.

"Oh noo!" Lizzie's anguished voice reached them. Ginger hurried to the kitchen with Felicia and Boss not far behind, and found Lizzie kneeling on the stone floor, picking up pieces of broken china. She looked up at Ginger with eyes full of tears, "I am so sorry, madam. I'll clean this up right away and you can take the cost of the plates from my earnings."

Ginger melted at the sight of her young maid in distress. "I will do no such thing," Ginger said as she walked over to Lizzie and gestured for her to stand up. "We have plenty of plates in the cupboards, but I have only one of you." She looked Lizzie in the eye. "You are quite obviously not yourself today, that is easy to see. Now tell me, what is the matter?"

Lizzie's eyes flashed with fear and embarrassment, darting to Mrs. Beasley who scowled at her from her position by the sink. "Oh no, I don't want to bother you with such things, madam. I...."

"Nonsense," Ginger said kindly. "I will judge for myself whether it's a bother." She placed a hand on Lizzie's shoulder. "Now come, let's spill the beans, shall we?"

Lizzie's trickle of tears became a torrent.

"It's my younger brother, Lewis." Lizzie's voice broke with anguish. "He's only eighteen."

Ginger's heart skipped a beat. "What's happened to Lewis?"

Lizzie struggled to get the words out. "He's been arrested!"

2

———

"Oh mercy." Ginger grasped at the string of pearls around her neck. "Arrested for what?" She leaned over to the countertop to get a tea towel and handed it to Lizzie.

"For stealing a goose from Collins' Butcher's shop," Lizzie sputtered, dabbing her eyes with the tea towel. "But he didn't do it! I know he didn't!"

Ginger caught the eye of her cook, Mrs. Beasley, whose girth filled the area in front of the sink. Her small eyes almost disappeared in her broad face as they narrowed in horror at the scene taking place before her.

"Mrs. Beasley," Ginger said with a smile, "I think Lizzie should sit down for a spell."

"Yes, madam." The cook, looking none too pleased, produced a chair, and Lizzie lowered herself into it.

"I know that shop," Felicia said. "It's over in Shepherds Bush, isn't it? One of the larger butcher's shops there, I think."

Lizzie twisted the tea towel with both hands. "Yes, that's the one. It's owned by Mr. Collins who brought charges against our Lewis. The thing is," Lizzie said, looking beseechingly at Ginger, "I *know* Lewis. He wouldn't *ever* steal anything. He has a heart as soft as the King's custard and is as honest as the day is long. I've never known him to ever tell a lie."

"What does Lewis say about it?" Ginger asked.

"I don't know why, but he's not saying anything at all!" Lizzie said in exasperation. "The police arrested him yesterday afternoon and are keeping him at the police station."

Ginger wasn't sure what the conditions were like at that jail, but she definitely didn't like the thought of this young man being kept there along with other, possibly dangerous criminals.

"One of the policemen let me talk to Lewis for just a few moments," Lizzie said. "The most frustrating thing about it is that Lewis is saying nothing in his defence!"

"You mean he doesn't deny it?" Ginger asked.

"Well, yes, he does deny he stole the goose, but when I asked him how he ended up with it, he says he just found it on our back step."

Ginger tucked a lock of her red bob behind her ear as she considered Lizzie's words. "Has anyone actually seen the goose in question?"

"We all did! Lewis came into the house carrying it." Lizzie nodded her pointy chin. "We all rejoiced, of course. Times are hard for us in our house, madam, not that I'm complaining." Her tired eyes appealed to Ginger. "I'm so grateful for this job. It's just that our father got laid off from his factory job, and my brother James, who worked as an automobile mechanic, injured his hand last month and hasn't been able to work. Lewis works as an apprentice at a printer's, and between him and me, we keep the roof over our heads. But even with our combined earnings, it certainly doesn't allow for such luxuries as a Christmas goose!"

"I see," Ginger said, her mind turning. "Lewis carried in a goose, and then what happened?"

"Well I...I put it in the pantry. We were going to cook it tomorrow. But two hours after we put the goose on the cold slab came a loud knock at the door. A policeman stood there with Mr. Collins. They said that a goose had gone missing from the shop and that it was our Lewis who took it. We were all in shock! They took the goose and put Lewis in *handcuffs*. Our mother is shattered."

This brought a fresh wave of tears from Lizzie as Ginger squeezed her hand.

"How do they know your goose came from their shop?" Felicia asked.

"At Christmas they always decorate their birds with a piece of green cloth around the ends of the legs to make them look festive. They do it with chickens and turkeys too. It's their trademark, they say. This goose had that same bit of decoration. I've no doubt the goose came from their storerooms, but I don't know how it got dropped off at our door."

"What led them to believe Lewis took it?" Ginger asked. "Did someone see him take it?"

Lizzie patted the twisted tea towel under her nose. "The man who worked behind the counter saw Lewis there. Then, a few minutes later both the goose and Lewis had disappeared."

Ginger shot a look at Felicia. She felt helpless, and she didn't like to see a member of her staff in such obvious distress. Yet, from her vantage point, it was entirely possible that the lad had stolen the goose. The temptation could be great for those falling on hard times. Ginger wished Lizzie had revealed her troubles earlier.

"I don't know what to do, madam!" Lizzie said. "We're all very upset over this and I fear for my mother's health. She's been so frail for a few years now and this could make it worse. She hasn't eaten anything since this all happened."

"Oh, dear child." Ginger squeezed Lizzie's hand again.

Perhaps it wouldn't hurt to ask a few questions at the butcher's shop, Ginger thought with some trepidation. But then, if it turned out that Lewis had stolen that goose, Ginger would have to be the bearer of the bad news.

What a frightfully sad way to start the Christmas holidays.

3
———————

It was early afternoon when Ginger, accompanied by Felicia, parked her white Crossley Sports Tourer across the street from Collins' Butcher's shop, just a short distance from the entrance to Shepherd's Bush underground station. Felicia, one hand gripping the door handle and the other against the dashboard, inhaled as if she was thankful to be alive. Ginger admitted to sliding a bit along the slippery roads and acknowledged the jarring bump of her tyres against the kerb as they came to an abrupt stop.

"Oh look," Ginger said, pointing a finger of her gloved hand towards a small brass band playing cheerful Christmas music, giving the whole street a festive ambience. The words "Salvation Army" were painted on a white wooden sign. Ginger, waving Felicia to follow her, went straight over to them and dropped some coins into their collection basket. They listened for a moment with Ginger smiling and even singing a few notes. After a rousing chorus of *Hark, the Herald Angels Sing*, Ginger applauded and then turned to walk to the butcher's shop.

Thankfully, the weather had lightened up a bit and the

sun had decided to make a rare appearance, making the day seem almost cheerful in Shepherd's Bush. Still, Ginger and Felicia had both bundled up in warm winter Parisian coats and hats trimmed with fox fur, and even though the cloth top was left up on the Crossley, it was a cold trip.

Ginger couldn't remember the last time she'd stepped inside a butcher's shop. Even in Boston, where she lived as a child on Beacon Hill, the servants of the house did all the shopping for food supplies, and this was true at Hartigan House today.

The bell rang overhead as they entered, and Ginger caught her breath at the strong smell of raw meat. Cuts of all kinds hung from hooks and were laid out on display in sprawling glass cases. The pungent smell of raw meat was pervasive.

"Good thing we left Boss behind!" she said.

Felicia agreed. "He'd be in either ecstasy or misery, or some poor blend of both."

Three male assistants, all dressed in white aprons, stood behind the counters located around the shop. Ginger counted fifteen customers—it was obviously a busy time for butcher's shops all over London—all of whom were bundled up in winter clothing, making little white clouds of breath vapor whenever they spoke. A cool temperature helped to preserve the meat while it was on display.

Ginger approached one of the men dressed in a white apron. A young man in his twenties, he wore thick clothing under the apron and had on a pair of woollen earmuffs. He finished with a customer who had bought a large goose, and Ginger noted the green cloth wrapped around the end of each of the bird's legs.

"Excuse me," she said with a smile. "I would like to speak to the manager. Is he on the premises?"

The young man looked at her with surprise, but then noticed her expensive-looking winter wear. "'E's out the back in 'is office, miss. Give me a moment an' I'll fetch 'im." He glanced appreciatively at Felicia and then left through a curtained door behind the counter.

A moment later, a stocky middle-aged man with a white butcher's hat on a balding head and a day's worth of grey whiskers on ruddy cheeks appeared. He wore round wire-framed spectacles, which he pulled off as he approached

"I'm Mrs. Reed," Ginger said with authority, "the wife of Chief Inspector Basil Reed." Ginger had gathered that mentioning Basil's name and title would not hurt even though her husband didn't yet know about any of this. "And this is Miss Felicia Gold. We're here on the business of my office, *Lady Gold Investigations*."

Her introduction caused the man's eyebrows to furrow together.

Ginger pressed on. "Is there somewhere we can talk in private?"

THE BUTCHER LED them down a small hallway and into a medium-sized, spartanly furnished office which was thankfully a few degrees warmer than the large shop. He gestured to two wooden chairs that faced a large oak desk. The walls were painted white and virtually unadorned, with no pictures save one: a wooden-framed portrait showing the butcher dressed in formal clothes standing unsmiling beside an attractive woman of about the same age. Beside them was a young lady in her teens with a winsome smile and curly hair.

"That's my family," Mr. Collins said as he noticed Ginger looking at the photograph.

"Very nice," Ginger returned. "Is it a family enterprise then? This shop, I mean."

"Yes, to some extent." The man cleared his throat. "My wife takes care of the house and I take care of the shop. We do quite well, you know."

Ginger sighed inwardly at the strange comment. Could it

have been a reaction to Ginger mentioning her title? Ginger sometimes found the distinction between classes in London society quite tiring. It was a barrier that had to be overcome again and again when dealing with people, especially when conducting investigations as Lady Gold. One never knew if one's title would cause someone to be defensive or cause them to let their guard down.

"I'm sure you do," she replied simply.

"It's a very busy time of year, as you can imagine. Our daughter, Frances, has just finished at school and she helps out here from time to time as well, with advertising and things like that. I know that's unusual for a young lady, but she insists, and I don't object. She seems to have quite a mind for business, that one. Besides, it's busy this time of year, and I need all the help I can get.

"Now then, Mrs. Reed. What can I do for you? You are obviously here about the business with the stolen goose."

"Yes, that's right."

"Then I'm afraid you have come here on a cold winter's day for no reason. The goose went missing and we know who took it. Therefore, he deserves to be in prison where he belongs, and I plan to press charges. I am afraid not even your husband, as important a man as he is, can bend the law in these kinds of matters."

There it was again, thought Ginger, that barely hidden antagonism.

"My husband would not dream of making an exception for anyone when it comes to the law, Mr. Collins. I am here simply to find out what happened in a bit more detail. Forgive me for saying it, sir, but it is your word against the young man's in question, isn't it?" The man narrowed his stare. Ginger continued, undaunted, "Lewis Weaver maintains his innocence. I want to know if he has any grounds for that. I do not want him in prison if he is wrongly accused. It's that simple."

The butcher snorted and leaned back in his chair with his beefy forearms behind his head. "What do you want to know then?"

"Who saw him take the goose?"

A moment of hesitation could be read in the man's eyes. Ginger guessed this question was not exactly what he had expected.

"Well... no one actually saw him but..."

"Oh well, isn't that surprising then? A young man is going to spend Christmas in a jail cell for a crime no one saw him commit." Ginger raised her eyebrows.

"No one *saw* him take it, but he was seen in our shop just moments before it went missing and it *was* found not two hours later at the Weavers' house, wasn't it?" The man leaned forward again in his chair and rapped his knuckles softly on his desk. "So, I ask you, Mrs. Reed, what is a fella like that doing in our shop? Do you know how often we get blokes like that in our shop to buy *anything* at all, much less an expensive goose like that?" His voice raised an octave. "Well, I can tell you. Since a goose like that equals about a week's wage for a lot of people...the answer is *never*. You have to ask yourself, Detective..."

Ginger cut him off, feeling her own temper rise. "So then, you must know him."

"No...no, I never said that. I don't know him." Mr. Collins shrugged in bewilderment at the question.

"Really? I thought since you went straight to the Weavers' house you must have known where he lived."

"No, I don't know him."

"Had he been here before then?" Ginger found herself feeling irritated both by the man's rudeness and by her own response to it. This was the Christmas season after all.

Mr. Collins hesitated, then, with a tired sigh, answered, "Yes, apparently he has been here before. But I've never seen him myself. It was one of my employees who recognised him and knew where he lived."

"I should like to speak to that man, please," Ginger said.

"Mrs. Reed, I actually think you have taken up enough of my time. Now since you are not actually a representative of the law, and I am a very busy man with a shop full of customers to take care of, I bid you and Miss Gold goodbye." He stood up from his desk.

"Who saw him, Mr. Collins?" Ginger's voice was firm as she put a hand on Felicia's arm to indicate they were not leaving until they got an answer.

The man sighed and shook his head. "It was Nels Stanwick. He was the one who realised that the goose was missing. He also remembered seeing Lewis in the shop."

"Thank you. We will go now and talk to him." Ginger and Felicia both stood to go.

"He's not here." The butcher nodded towards the door. "His shift ended about an hour ago. Good day, madam."

In a huff, Mr. Collins disappeared through a door at the back. The shop was in a sudden lull, with only a handful of customers in the room.

"What are we going to do?" Felicia said softly. "Shall we perhaps visit Lewis Weaver?"

"In time," Ginger said. She turned to the assistant they had talked to earlier, now busy wiping down a metal countertop.

"Excuse me, I'm looking for Mr. Stanwick," Ginger said. "Do you know where I can find him?"

The man paused and thought for a moment. "I think 'e left about an hour ago. That's when 'is shift ends 'ere."

Ginger looked at her watch. "It is now almost two p.m. He only works until one?"

"On most days. Nels is part of the early morning crew that helps bring the meat out of the ice safe to ready it for display."

"Did he finish at one p.m. yesterday?"

"Yes, I think so."

Ginger thought for a moment. "Do you happen to know where this man lives?"

"No, but I know where 'e'll be tonight. The lad works at Selfridges department store as a lift operator every day during the Christmas season starting at five p.m."

4

———

The police station was a large red-brick building three storeys high built right on the corner of two busy streets. It seemed to Ginger it would be an imposing place for an eighteen-year old. Fortunately, it was only a short fifteen-minute drive from the butcher's shop and the sun had now had a chance to warm up the air a little bit, so driving was a bit more tolerable than earlier in the day. Ginger wasn't sure if they would be allowed in to see Lewis, but if not, she intended to phone Scotland Yard to see if Basil could gain them entrance on his authority. However, a fortuitous meeting occurred just as Ginger and Felicia approached the double entrance doors to the reception office.

A familiar voice rang out from across the street. "Well I'll be. If it ain't Lady Gold from the dress shop!"

The cheerful, portly figure of Inspector Sanders trundled towards them, his round cheeks flushed red from the cold and his large moustache lightly frosted. Ginger had made his acquaintance a few months earlier when he became involved in solving a theft case at Ginger's dress shop, *Feathers & Flair*. The police officer had become quite a source of amusement for the ladies working there, with his swaggering personality and winsome mannerisms, all of which the ladies found endearing.

"Hello, Inspector Sanders," Ginger returned, smiling. "What a pleasure to see you again." She gestured to Felicia. "You remember my sister-in-law, Miss Gold?"

"Of course!" He regarded Felicia with merry, bright-blue eyes and then bowed slightly, tipping his hat. "A pleasure to see you again, miss.

"If yer don't mind me askin', wot are you lovely ladies going into a rough place like this for? You should be out shopping or enjoying some puddin'."

"We are here to see a young man incarcerated yesterday on charges of stealing goods from a butcher's shop," Ginger said, then solemnly added, "I have some reservations about the charges and would like to go and get to the bottom of the matter."

Inspector Sanders' bushy brows arched in question. "You have a note from a judge, then?"

Ginger pursed her lips, to which lipstick had been newly applied in the motorcar. "I'm afraid not."

"Hmm." Inspector Sanders stroked his moustache and rocked back and forth on his heels. "Normally, you're not allowed to go in t' visit prisoners waiting to be charged, madam. Not without proper permission from t' judge."

"I see," Ginger said, then employed a measure of charm. "Do you think you could help us, Inspector?"

Felicia took it a step further by fluttering her eyelashes and taking the officer's arm. "It would mean so much."

Ginger shot Felicia a look. Sometimes her sister-in-law didn't know where to draw the line!

However, her antics appeared to do their work. The inspector sniffed, cleared his throat, rubbed his chin, and looked off into the distance as if pondering one of life's deep mysteries.

"They do know me here at this station. I've brought in my

fair share of dastardly malefactors, I 'ave." He rocked again on his heels. "An' the officer in charge 'as asked me to pose as Father Christmas this year at a children's charity event."

"Oh, you would be wonderful at that!" Ginger couldn't help but say.

"I was last year, Mrs. Reed. They couldn't get enough of me, the little nippers. Ha! I 'ad 'em all eatin' out of me 'ands, I did. God Bless all o' them little tykes." He set his blue-eyed gaze on both Ginger and Felicia for a moment and then pivoted towards the building. "C'mon, let's see if we can get you a meetin'."

Ginger and Felicia sat in the waiting room of the reception area while Inspector Sanders disappeared down a hallway, a stern resolution in his stride. A few minutes later he came back followed by a dour-looking man with greying sideburns, who introduced himself as the officer in charge.

"I can let you in to one of our meeting rooms and bring the prisoner to you," he said, his gaze drawn to the flirtatious Felicia. "It's not our usual policy without written permission, but... well, the inspector here can be quite persuasive."

"As any good detective should be!" Inspector Sanders said with some amount of swagger. "Well, m'ladies, I've business 'ere I need to attend to, if you'll excuse me."

They thanked him profusely and said their goodbyes after which the governor led them into a room with a barred window overlooking a large inner courtyard, wet with dirty snow. They sat on wooden chairs that were sitting around a small table, as they waited for Lewis Weaver to be fetched.

A short while later, a man wearing a sargeant's uniform entered. He was accompanied by a bedraggled-looking youth, Lewis Weaver, who had dark, unkempt hair, hazel eyes, and a slight build. He stared at Ginger and Felicia in confusion. Ginger made quick introductions.

"Ah, yes, Lizzie speaks highly of you, madam," Lewis said. "But surely she didn't ask you—"

"No, we're here of our own accord," Ginger said. "Lizzie is part of my household, and I'm very fond of her."

"Oh. I see."

"Are you all right?" Ginger asked.

Lewis glanced at Ginger with some trepidation.

"Yes. I'm okay. Didn't sleep a wink, but well and fed well enough."

"I told Lizzie that I was willing to look into the matter of your arrest," Ginger said. "Is there anything you can tell me that could lead to proof of your innocence?"

"I... don't know what to say, Mrs. Reed. I found the goose on our back step wrapped in a blanket like a baby. I brought it into the house and a short time later Mr. Collins was there with a police constable. That's really all I know."

Ginger let out a slow breath. This case was perplexing.

Lewis' timidity fell away as he stared Ginger in the eye. "I promise you, madam, I didn't steal it."

If the young man was lying, he was very good at it.

"You were seen at the shop just before the goose was taken," Ginger said.

At that statement the boy suddenly looked away for a moment, then with a quiet voice, admitted, "I... yes. I was there."

With a soft voice, Ginger asked, "Can you tell us what you were doing there if you weren't going to buy anything?"

He stared at his own twiddling thumbs, and after a long pause said, "I was there to see Frances."

"Frances Collins?" Ginger confirmed. "You are involved with the butcher's daughter?"

His lips tightened as he dropped his chin.

"Let's be clear," Ginger continued, "do you mean to say you are romantically involved?"

Lewis Weaver blushed, embarrassed. "We are fond of each other. I have seen her on a few occasions."

Probably understatements, Ginger thought.

"How did the two of you meet?" Felicia said. "No offence, but I can't imagine you run in the same circles."

Ginger thought Felicia's comment was rather blunt, but she did have a point. Frances Collins, because she was from a successful middle-class family that ran a prominent business, wouldn't normally be associated with someone like Lewis Weaver, from the lower working class. They were breaking societal norms, though, Ginger thought ruefully, they certainly were not the first young people to do so.

"We met at the printer's where I work," Lewis replied. "She helps out her father sometimes an' manages all th' advertisements for the butcher's shop, especially in the busy Christmas season. We just sort of...you know, got along well and soon we were meeting each other outside of shop hours."

"I'm correct in stating that you were at the butcher's shop yesterday to call on young Miss Collins?"

"Yes, well, I wanted to surprise her. I knew she would finish work around then. I thought we could go for a walk or somefin'. The day was warmer than the others, and I was finished at work for the day."

"And... did that happen? Did you meet her?"

"No... I mean, she wasn't there. I usually wait for her in the back lane behind the shop. But yesterday she must've left early. As I said, she didn't know I was comin'.'"

"Then you went into the shop?" Felicia asked.

"Yes, to see if Frances was maybe working there." He shook his head forlornly. "But she wasn't."

"But you were seen, apparently," Ginger said. "Is there anyone at the shop who would know where you lived?"

"I don't think so. I don't know anyone there besides Frances."

Ginger shared a look with Felicia. "It remains a mystery then, of how Mr. Collins' employee knew where to direct the police constable."

"We have to talk to Frances Collins," Felicia stated.

"I agree," Ginger said, "but I'm certain Mr. Collins won't condone that." She caught Lewis' tired gaze. "We'll have to find a way to do it without his consent. Any ideas, Mr. Weaver?"

Lewis Weaver pinched his eyes together as he thought. When he opened them, he said, "Every morning at around ten she leaves the shop to run errands for her father. She often uses the underground station right across from the shop. Shepherd's Bush station."

"That's where we'll be tomorrow morning, first thing." Ginger sighed and then looked at her watch. "Time to go." She grinned at Felicia. "In the meantime, we'll see if the managers of Selfridges have outdone themselves this year with their Christmas decorations."

5

____

Ginger knew all about *Selfridges Department Store* and had visited it many times. When retail magnate Harry Selfridge had decided to build Europe's biggest department store in 1905, he'd had the radical notion that one could shop for pleasure rather than just out of necessity. This concept was, of course, something that Ginger Gold, owner of *Feathers & Flair boutique dress shop*, wholeheartedly agreed with. But at the time, scarcely twenty years ago, it had been a novel concept, and no one really knew how it would go down in London. In America, of course, people had already embraced the idea with huge department stores like *Fields* in Chicago and *Macy's* in Herald Square, New York City.

It was a bold, new idea for shopping, where London's lower and middle classes could momentarily escape the heavily layered class structure of society to shop alongside each other as well as those from the upper class. Ginger always found that gloriously refreshing.

She had not yet gone to Selfridges this Christmas season and actually relished the opportunity to do it. She had sent Lizzie there on occasion for shopping errands, most recently to buy Christmas presents for the staff at Hartigan House, but had not been there herself in months.

It was always a feast for the senses at Christmastime and this year was certainly no different at Selfridges. The decorations throughout the massive complex were glittering brightly, with lights hanging along the walls of the massive corridors. Musicians could be seen and heard playing joyful carols in practically every other corner. Huge Christmas trees with sparkling lights were set up, dwarfed by high ceilings and open vistas that were a main feature of the store's neo-classical architecture. One of the hallmarks of Selfridges was that many of the goods were stacked up in colourful, tall displays for people to touch and smell instead of being encased in glass display cases. 'Aladdin's cave' was the term often used to describe the place by many. The owner wanted the shopping experience to be very tactile and participatory, a spectacle that the shopper took part in. Ginger could smell the scents of perfumes from the huge ground-floor cosmetic and perfume section wafting through the building as soon as they entered.

"Now, Felicia, let's remain resolute!" Ginger said. "We are strong ladies. We *can* walk through this entire section without stopping!" Felicia moaned in dissent as Ginger tugged on her arm, though Ginger had to admit that she was saying this more to herself then to Felicia. She would have dearly loved to sample some of those new Parisian fragrances that she had heard about from some of the ladies at Feathers & Flair. She wondered about buying Basil a case of expensive cigars, or maybe some French brandy.

No time for that now.

As Ginger and Felicia slowly made their way through the busy crowds of Christmas shoppers, they saw on the right that there was a hair salon, and on the left, a large restaurant with a wide, open front entrance. Just a few shops down there was an art gallery next to a concierge counter where one could book train or theatre tickets.

They slowly made their way to the centre of the building where there was a series of nine very ornate lifts to service the five above-ground and three below-ground shopping levels. Each lift had its own lift operator. Most of the time, they were young ladies, dressed in crisp white knickerbockers, jackets, gloves, and hats, standing to attention ready to manually operate the lifts for shoppers. During the busy Christmas season, however, there were occasionally also young men operating the lifts. At the moment, five of the lifts were in transit. Out of the four lift attendants standing there, one was male. Ginger and Felicia approached him.

"Excuse me," Ginger said, "we are looking for Nels Stanwick."

The young man furrowed his eyebrows and looked at them both, "Yes, that's me."

He was in his twenties and very Nordic looking, with blond hair and blue eyes and a solid build. Ginger guessed that he would have been considered quite handsome to young ladies of his age, especially dressed in the smart white uniform. But Ginger noticed his eyes held a certain look of hardness which gave the feeling that he might be capable of being unfeeling, or even cruel at times.

"I'm Lady Gold of Lady Gold Investigations and this is Miss Felicia Gold." As the lift attendant was rather nice to look at, Felicia grinned flirtatiously. "Hello," she said softly.

Ginger rolled her eyes, then turned her attention to the young man. "Mr. Stanwick, do you mind if we ask you a few questions."

"I suppose not."

"We understand you saw Lewis Weaver at Collins' Butcher's shop yesterday."

Mr. Stanwick stiffened. "That's right, I did. Just before that goose went missin'."

Just then a man and a woman accompanied by two young children approached the lift.

Nels Stanwick looked relieved at the interruption. "Up or down?" he asked politely.

"Up, to the main restaurant, if you please," replied the man as he and his family stepped into the lift.

Ginger decided to step in as well, and Felicia followed. This made the lift quite cramped and Ginger made a point of standing right next to Nels Stanwick. She didn't know if it would make him nervous, but if so, that would be all right with her. As the lift started, the two children both pointed at the translucently lit ceiling. "We're going up!" one of them cried. This made both parents chuckle. Ginger kept her eyes fixed on Nels Stanwick whose expression remained inscrutable despite her steadfast gaze.

When the door opened to the expansive fourth-floor restaurant, the family got out and so did Nels Stanwick. Ginger and Felicia stepped out as well. Nels Stanwick stepped to the left of the lift entrance, waiting for the next customers, though at the moment there were none waiting to board.

"Look, I can't talk right now," he muttered with some annoyance.

"Won't take a moment," Ginger replied. "How do you know him, Lewis Weaver, I mean?"

"Well I... I don't really know him."

"But you recognised him. And then you told the police where he lived, isn't that so?"

A look of uncertainty came into the young man's eyes. He glanced around the store, averting his eyes from Ginger's.

" 'E comes pokin' around," he said finally. "I told Mr. Collins about 'im alright. 'Im and Frances go sneakin' out together to who knows where."

Aha, Ginger thought. She knew jealousy when she saw it.

Felicia did too. "Did that bother you, Mr. Stanwick?" she asked, a lilt of a tease to her voice.

Nels Stanwick threw Felicia a scornful look and then quickly looked around in case customers were watching.

Ginger wanted to head off any argument between the two straight away. "And how did you know where he lives?"

Again, there was a pause. The poor lad hadn't known he was going to be asked these hard questions today, Ginger thought.

"I followed 'em one day, din't I?" he said, his gaze darting around the store again. "Mr. Collins knew about it and was in full agreement. 'E don't want 'im comin' around to see 'is daughter neither. So, I followed Mr. Weaver 'ome one day after he dropped off Frances."

"And how well do you know the young Miss Collins?" Ginger asked.

"I know 'er well enough. An' she knows me. And," he added defensively, "if it were up to Mr. Collins, we might know each other even better."

"Of course," Ginger said wryly. She didn't know if that was true or just wishful thinking on the part of Nels Stanwick.

"How was it noticed that the goose was missing?" Felicia asked. "Was it stolen from the displays?"

"No, it went missing from one of th' back storerooms. Lewis Weaver would 'ave known 'ow to get in there unnoticed, I reckon."

"And who noticed it had gone?" Ginger asked.

"Well, I did. I'm one of th' ones responsible for keeping track, as well as preparing displays for th' day."

Their conversation was stilted by another group of shoppers approaching the lift.

"I'm now sayin' good day to you, ladies." Nels Stanwick doffed his white cap and then turned to the new customers. "Down we go then?"

"I WONDER if Mr. Stanwick took the goose and put it on the Weavers' back step," Ginger said, as they stepped back onto Oxford Street and headed towards the Crossley.

Felicia snorted in response. "Then he blamed it on Lewis Weaver!"

"It's definitely a possibility." They climbed into the car and Ginger put it into gear and pulled away.

"What do we do now then?" Felicia asked. "How can we prove that?"

"Nothing more to be done today, I suppose." Ginger looked at her watch again as she drove. The butcher's shop was going to be closing very soon. "I'm afraid we will have to leave it for tomorrow, even though it means Lewis must spend another day in custody."

6

The next morning, Ginger tasked Felicia with tying up loose ends at the office, which Felicia was happy to do. She'd much rather use the quiet to work on the new mystery book she was writing and avoided "waiting about" type of assignments as they were "too boring".

Instead, Ginger took Scout with her to the butcher's shop. She also wanted to return to Selfridges before they closed. While she and Felicia were there the day before, she'd spied a very nice pair of tweed trousers that were just about Scout's size and would make a very nice early Christmas present in addition to the new cap she had already bought him and wrapped for Christmas morning. But she wanted to make sure the trousers fit him first. Her prepubescent ward had been going through a bit of a period of rapid growth recently and was outgrowing some of his clothes. It would be hard to shop for clothes for him now unless he was present.

When Ginger had first met Scout, he was an underfed little waif working aboard the SS *Rosa* steamship as an animal minder for pets of the upper class on the long voyage from Boston to Liverpool. The orphaned boy had found a place in her heart almost immediately and she had eventually taken on the role of being his legal guardian. Now, just a few years later, she planned to go through the adoption process necessary to make him a permanent member of the family. Ginger had never had one moment of regret for what some people from the upper class would sniff at. The lad was smart, good-natured, loving, and even at his young age, was very appreciative of the better life that had been afforded him. Ginger was strict but gentle with him and the lad responded well. After a time, he'd become a beloved member of the Hartigan House household, having also forged a good relationship with Basil after she and he had wed.

It was just a few minutes before 10 a.m. when Ginger slowed to find a parking spot just near the Shepherd's Bush underground station, very close to where they had parked the day before. The entrance to Collins' Butcher's shop could be seen just on the left side of the street a bit further down. Ginger was just lining up the Crossley to park when she happened to glance down the street and see what looked very much like Frances Collins, from the picture she had seen in Mr. Collins' office, with curly hair escaping a winter cloche hat. Frances Collins skipped quickly across the junction, making her way across the street and into the station. If she reached her train, Ginger would lose her, and she hadn't even parked yet.

"Oh mercy!"

"Wot is it?" asked Scout, looking at her with wide eyes and a large toothy grin.

"See that girl with the curly hair, crossing the street? That's the girl I mean to talk to, but it looks like I won't be able to catch—"

In a flash, Scout jumped out of the Crossley and ran around the car onto the pavement. "Don't you worry, missus. I'll stop her from gettin' on th' train." He sprinted through the crowd, towards the figure of Frances Collins who was just now entering the main doors of the station.

"Good boy, Scout!" Ginger said as she carefully manoeuvred the Crossley into a tight parking spot and stepped out of the motorcar.

She hurried to the main doors and entered the station, searching for the two young people amidst the crowd. At first, she despaired that perhaps even Scout could not have found the girl in the bustling train station, but after a few moments, she spotted Frances Collins standing against a far wall. Her face showed utter bafflement as she stared down at a much shorter Scout who was waving his arms in the air and saying God knew what to keep her from continuing on her way.

"Thank you, Scout!" Ginger said as she approached the two. "So sorry. Miss Collins is it?" Ginger extended her hand.

"Y...yes, it is. This lad says you have something important to talk to me about." The girl shook Ginger's gloved hand with a bewildered expression.

"Miss Collins, I'm Mrs. Reed. This young man's name is Scout and he is in my care as my ward." Ginger smiled at the girl warmly. She did not want to alarm her or give the girl any reason to be intimidated. "Lizzie Weaver is in my employ."

"Oh..." The girl said simply as her eyes widened with recognition at the Weaver name.

Ginger pressed on. "I'm looking into the matter of Lewis Weaver's recent arrest, and I was hoping you might be able to shed some light on a few things."

The girl looked stunned for a moment and Ginger worried that she might indeed be too frightened by the whole strange encounter to give them any information.

"It's okay, miss," Scout piped up. "The missus is as kind of a lady you'll ever find 'ere in this ol' town." His face beamed with pride. Ginger had to hold in a chuckle at her young ward's effusiveness and at his choice of words: *This ol' town.*

Scout sagely nodded his head while waving his hand at Ginger. "I reckon you can be straight wiv 'er alright."

"Um...Yes, I know Lewis," Frances said as she looked back and forth from Scout to Ginger. "Is he all right?"

"As well as can be expected," Ginger said. "Can we sit down and talk for a moment?" She pointed at a bench that was currently unoccupied. Scout immediately ran over to it to stop anyone else from sitting on it and waited for them.

"Lizzie came to me quite upset yesterday," Ginger said as they sat down. Scout jumped up to make room and then stood a few feet away, sometimes nodding cheerfully at people as they passed by if they happened to notice him standing there.

"As you are probably aware," Ginger continued, "Lewis was arrested for stealing a goose from your father's shop."

The girl remained silent, her face a veil of sadness.

"Lewis said that you two are... friends?"

Frances nodded her head meekly.

"Did you see anything yesterday?" Ginger asked gently. "Apparently, he came to the butcher's shop to visit you." Frances' lower lip began to quiver.

"I'd already gone," she finally said, her voice cracking. "But they told me about it afterwards."

Her eyes welled up with tears and Scout reached into his pocket and produced a clean cloth handkerchief and handed it to her. "There, there, miss." He patted her on the shoulder. "Here y' go. It's okay. I know it's 'ard t' believe, me bein' a man an' all, but I've shed a few meself on occasion."

Ginger couldn't help the proud smile that formed on her face. It was just a simple gesture of empathy from a young lad, but the effect was powerful. Frances Collins suddenly burst into tears, buried her face in her hands, and leaned forward. Ginger put her arm around her.

"There now, dear girl," Ginger cooed.

Frances Collins wept uncontrollably, drawing the stare of a few passers-by. Eventually, she managed to pull herself together. "It's all my fault!" She kneaded Scout's handkerchief in her trembling fingers.

"How could that be?" Ginger asked quietly.

"Lewis didn't take that goose. I did!" Her confession brought a fresh wave of tears, and she buried her face once again in her hands.

Ginger and Scout exchanged a look. Scout just shrugged while continuing to pat the girl on the shoulder.

"You mean, you stole it to give it to the Weaver family?" Ginger asked. The girl nodded vigorously.

"But why?" Ginger was flummoxed. "If you wanted to give the family a goose, you could have just asked your father."

"I did!" Frances said. "But he refused to let me do it. He said I should have nothing to do with that family. But that's just being cruel, isn't it? So out of spite, I decided to do it anyway. I just didn't think anyone would notice the bird was missing so soon. I also didn't count on Lewis coming into the shop."

Frances stared at Ginger with reddened eyes, new tears forming. "That blasted Nels! He's the one who said that Lewis did it. He's the one my father believes."

"But surely you told your father what you did?"

"Of course I did! When I found out that they had arrested poor Lewis, I was beside myself. I confessed right away to my father, but he wouldn't believe me. He told me I was just protecting Lewis out of pity!" She spat out the last word, her tears turning angry. "I don't pity Lewis. I love him!"

There it was, Ginger thought. Motive for Mr. Collins to frame a man for thievery.

Frances continued to dab at her eyes. "Father forbade me to go to the police. Oh my goodness, I haven't slept or eaten since I found out they'd arrested him."

7

———

It was mid-morning when Ginger and Scout entered the butcher's shop, threading a path through the crowded room and, without hesitation, headed straight for the back rooms behind the counters.

One of the shop assistants looked at her in surprise as she breezed past him with Scout behind her, struggling to keep up with her longer strides. "Can I help you, miss?"

Ginger ignored the man, and walked right through the door and down the hall to Mr. Collins' office, finding him at his desk engrossed in paperwork. Upon seeing Ginger at his door, he removed his wire-framed spectacles, scowled, and leaned back in his chair.

"Alright, Lady Gold, or Mrs. Reed, or whatever your name is. What's it this time?"

"You can call me Mrs. Reed." Ginger stood in the doorway with Scout who peered around the room with curiosity. "Your daughter is rather upset."

Mr. Collins glared. "When did you talk to Frances?"

"Just now at the underground station. It was an informative conversation to say the least."

The burly shopkeeper leaned forward in his chair. "I will thank you to leave my daughter alone!"

"And I will thank you to be forthright in your conversations. How convenient that you omitted the fact that it was your *daughter* who placed that goose on the back doorstep of the Weavers' house."

"She did not! She's only saying that to protect that young ne'er do well."

"Mr. Lewis Weaver holds down a respectable job at a printer's and is a decent, upright citizen. And now, simply because you don't believe your own daughter, you have caused an innocent man to be arrested, and at Christmastime!"

Mr. Collins, his bulbous face as red as a Christmas ornament, jumped to his feet. "How dare you stick your nose in my family's business!"

"I have absolutely no desire to be involved in your *family* affairs, Mr. Collins, but what you have done here against the *Weaver* household is unconscionable. I won't let it stand."

Mr. Collins pointed a stubby finger towards the door, but before he could get the words out demanding they leave, Ginger said, "Does your daughter have a history of lying?"

"What the devil?" Mr. Collins blustered. "Of course not!"

Ginger softened her expression. "I thought as much. I suspect her character to be very sincere in nature, and she obviously has a generous heart to go along with it. It baffles me, Mr. Collins, as to why you won't believe her when she tells you something of such importance. You must agree that sending an innocent man to prison is not a trivial matter. You should *at least* give your own daughter's words careful consideration. That girl is in extreme anguish right now. I would bet my best imported French hat that she's telling the truth!"

Scout nodded vigorously and spouted in agreement, "She ain't no liar, that one."

Mr. Collins stared at Scout for a moment, mouth dropping open. "Who are...?" Then he shook his head and looked up at

Ginger again. "My daughter thinks she's in love with that lad. It's blinded her."

Ginger didn't want to get into a debate about the follies of young love. She asked, "I'm curious to know what your wife thinks of it all?"

Mr. Collins blew air out of his cheeks. "She believes Frances."

"A perceptive lady."

The butcher lowered himself back into his seat, but his mouth remained pinched in an expression of stubborn refusal. Ginger sighed. She had no choice but to use the next weapon from her arsenal.

"Mr. Collins, I don't know if you are aware that I own Feathers & Flair, a fine dress shop on Regent Street?"

"So? What is that to me?"

"I would wager that many of my customers, all of whom are from well-to-do families, and some of whom own large estates, send their servants to your shop for their meat because of the variety you have, and certainly because of your fine reputation. Do you think that might be true?"

"Well, yes, I imagine that..."

"Ladies love to talk about all kinds of things while they are browsing the latest fashions."

The butcher worked his lips. "Just what are you getting at?"

Ginger ignored the question. "You know, it's interesting, last week I noticed signs for a brand-new, and very large butcher's shop going up just a few streets from here. *Lorenzo's* I think it's called. Are you familiar with it?"

Mr. Collins stared at her with a steely expression.

"Two Italian families I believe," Ginger said. "And a bakery right next door that will feature fine Italian pastries. Two shops owned by close relatives! Imagine that! You like pastries, don't you, Scout?"

"I do, missus, I do!"

"This new opening will be quite a topic of conversation in our shop, I would guess. Wouldn't you agree, Mr. Collins?"

Mr. Collins dropped his pen onto his desk, his shoulders slumping as he let out a long sigh.

"What do you want, Mrs. Reed?"

"I want Mr. Weaver released this afternoon, and the largest goose you have in the shop sent to his family immediately."

8

———

Ginger and Scout pulled away from the kerb and headed towards Oxford Street. There was just enough afternoon left for a stop at Selfridges before heading back to Hartigan House.

"Do Italians really make good pastries?" Scout asked after several moments of silence. The boy had been deep in thought.

"Oh my, yes. In fact, I think I might pick up some struffoli while we are at Selfridges."

"I love strawferlee!" The lad clapped his hands together, then grew quiet again. After a moment, he asked, "What is strawferlee?"

Ginger smiled. "Struffoli are little dough balls that have been deep fried, soaked in honey, and then sprinkled with bits of fine chocolate or candied fruit."

The lad gasped and stared, his eyes as wide as mince pies.

"In fact, I believe you deserve some struffoli tonight. We'll eat them beside the Christmas tree after we sing carols. Does that sound good?"

Scout closed his eyes and leaned back against the seat of the Crossley. "I am goin' t' start imaginin' that taste in my mouf right now."

Ginger laughed, "Me too."

"Can I give Boss some strawferlee?"

"Perhaps just a tiny bit. We don't want him getting fat!" She smiled. "By the way, thank you for helping me today there at the underground station."

"Ah, it was nothin'. I like that Miss Frances Collins. She 'as a good 'eart."

Ginger nodded in agreement.

"Do you fink it's goin' t' be alright? Is Mr. Collins goin' to let Lizzie's bruvver out of jail?"

"Oh yes, I think that will happen this afternoon."

Selfridges was even busier than it had been the day before and it took longer than Ginger had expected to find the right trousers for her young charge. They had picked up a large bag of Italian pastries at one of the bakery sections of the store, along with a bag of sweets and more decorations for the Christmas tree. They had stopped to listen to a small group of carol-singers singing just outside the bakery department for a few minutes, but Ginger was anxious to get home and let Lizzie know that her brother would be home soon.

As Ginger pulled the Crossley into the large detached garage at Hartigan House, her heart began to finally feel some anticipation for a quiet Christmas at home with her family.

"It's the season to be jolly they say, Scout," she said cheerily as they walked towards the entrance of the house, arms laden with shopping bags, feet crunching on a thin blanket of fallen snow.

"I am feelin' very jolly alright, missus. I can smell the food already!"

Lizzie rushed to meet them. "Madam! I don't know how you did it, but we've heard from Lewis and they're letting him go!"

Ginger smiled, feeling alight with Christmas good cheer. "That's fantastic news, Lizzie. Now why don't you go home to your family."

Lizzie brightened further. "Are you sure? Mrs. Beasley—"

"You leave Mrs. Beasley to me," Ginger said. "Now, go on."

"Thank you, madam, and Merry Christmas!"

WANT MORE GINGER GOLD? Check out the entire murder mystery series HERE.

MURDER AT HYDE PARK
The Ginger Gold Mysteries Book # 14

Murder's a fashion faux pas. . .

THE SUMMER of 1926 brings high fashion to Hyde Park. Ginger's Regent Street dress shop, Feathers & Flair, is a major sponsor, and when top designer Coco Chanel makes an appearance, the London fashion scene lights up.

Until a model's body is found and Miss Chanel is suspected of murder. The fashion icon hires Lady Gold Investigations to clear her name, but can Ginger discover the murderer before becoming a dead mannequin herself?

Buy on Amazon or read FREE with Kindle Unlimited!

Check out the new spin off series The Rosa Reed Mysteries!

Murder's all wet!

It's 1956 and WPC (Woman Police Constable) Rosa Reed has left her groom at the altar in London. Time spent with her American cousins in Santa Bonita, California is exactly what she needs to get back on her feet, though the last thing she expected was to get entangled in another murder case!

If you love early rock & roll, poodle skirts, clever who-dun-its, a charming cat and an even more charming detective, you're going to love this new series!

Buy on Amazon or read FREE with Kindle Unlimited!

**LADY GOLD INVESTIGATES (Ginger Gold companion
short stories)**

Volume 1

Volume 2

Volume 3

Volume 4

**HIGGINS & HAWKE MYSTERY SERIES (cozy 1930s
historical)**

*The 1930s meets Rizzoli & Isles in this friendship depression era cozy
mystery series.*

Death at the Tavern

Death on the Tower

Death on Hanover

THE ROSA REED MYSTERIES

(1950s cozy historical)

Murder at High Tide

Murder on the Boardwalk

Murder at the Bomb Shelter

Murder on Location

Murder and Rock 'n Roll

Murder at the Races

Murder at the Dude Ranch

**A NURSERY RHYME MYSTERY
SERIES(mystery/sci fi)**

*Marlow finds himself teamed up with intelligent and savvy Sage
Farrell, a girl so far out of his league he feels blinded in her presence -*

literally - damned glasses! Together they work to find the identity of @gingerbreadman. Can they stop the killer before he strikes again?

Gingerbread Man

Life Is but a Dream

Hickory Dickory Dock

Twinkle Little Star

THE PERCEPTION TRILOGY (YA dystopian mystery)

Zoe Vanderveen is a GAP—a genetically altered person. She lives in the security of a walled city on prime water-front property along side other equally beautiful people with extended life spans. Her brother Liam is missing. Noah Brody, a boy on the outside, is the only one who can help ∼ but can she trust him?

Perception

Volition

Contrition

LIGHT & LOVE (sweet romance)

Set in the dazzling charm of Europe, follow Katja, Gabriella, Eva, Anna and Belle as they find strength, hope and love.

Sing me a Love Song

Your Love is Sweet

In Light of Us

Lying in Starlight

PLAYING WITH MATCHES (WW2 history/romance)

A sobering but hopeful journey about how one young German boy copes with the war and propaganda. Based on true events.

A Piece of Blue String (companion short story)

THE CLOCKWISE COLLECTION (YA time travel romance)

Casey Donovan has issues: hair, height and uncontrollable trips to the 19th century! And now this ~ she's accidentally taken Nate Mackenzie, the cutest boy in the school, back in time. Awkward.

Clockwise

Clockwiser

Like Clockwork

Counter Clockwise

Clockwork Crazy

Clocked (companion novella)

Standalones

Seaweed

Love, Tink

ABOUT THE AUTHORS

Lee Strauss is a USA TODAY bestselling author of The Ginger Gold Mysteries series, The Higgins & Hawke Mystery series, The Rosa Reed Mystery series (cozy historical mysteries), A Nursery Rhyme Mystery series (mystery suspense), The Perception series (young adult dystopian), The Light & Love series (sweet romance), The Clockwise Collection (YA time travel romance), and young adult historical fiction with over a million books read. She has titles published in German, Spanish and Korean, and a growing audio library.

When Lee's not writing or reading she likes to cycle, hike, and stare at the ocean. She loves to drink caffè lattes and red wines in exotic places, and eat dark chocolate anywhere.

For more info on books by Lee Strauss and her social media links, visit leestraussbooks.com. To make sure you don't miss the next new release, be sure to sign up for her readers' list!

Join my FACEBOOK READERS GROUP for fun discussions and first-to-know exclusives!

Norm Strauss is a singer-songwriter and performing artist who's seen the stage of The Voice of Germany. Short story writing is a new passion he shares with his wife Lee Strauss. Find out more at norm@normstrauss.com

www.leestraussbooks.com
leestraussbooks@gmail.com